A CERTAIN SMILE

Freya has been made redundant and
her high-flying boyfriend, Jay, is pres-
surising her to join him in London.
But this would mean her leaving the
place her heart lies — her home in
the New Forest. And there are so
many things to consider: her friends,
her small cottage and her adorable,
little dog Henri . . . and there's a
certain dog walker with good legs
and a friendly smile. Freya knows
that she'd miss saying 'good morning'
to him too.

BETH JAMES

A CERTAIN SMILE

Complete and Unabridged

LINFORD
Leicester

First published in Great Britain in 2011

First Linford Edition
published 2012

British Library CIP Data

James, Beth.
    A certain smile. - - (Linford romance library)
    1. Love stories.
    2. Large type books.
    I. Title II. Series
    823.9'2–dc23

    ISBN 978–1–4448–1289–3

Published by
F. A. Thorpe (Publishing)
Anstey, Leicestershire
Set by Words & Graphics Ltd.
Anstey, Leicestershire
Printed and bound in Great Britain by
T. J. International Ltd., Padstow, Cornwall

This book is printed on acid-free paper

1

'Henri, come!' Freya watched with pride as the little King Charles spaniel obediently turned and trotted towards her.

'No need to look so indignant,' she said bending to tickle behind her dog's silky black ears. 'We have to keep an eye on each other you and me.'

Henri didn't look too impressed as with an 'Oh, is that all?' expression over her shoulder she set off again to sniff for new discoveries that might be lurking in the path verge.

Trying to dispel the anxious feeling that was clouding the back of her mind, Freya dug her hands deep into her pockets and looked about her. The New Forest was just about waking up. Dew was sparkling on the first fresh green growth on the bushes and the ground beneath her feet was spongy with moss. Soon there would be a riot of hawthorn and blackthorn blossom between the majestic oaks, beeches and birches that predominated in the beautiful woodland.

It was a stunning and peaceful area and she was incredibly lucky to live here she thought to herself, for maybe the thousandth time.

That's why it would be terrible to have to move away, persisted a small voice at the back of her mind.

As she emerged from the woodland path onto the more open heathland, the slanting rays of the early morning sun hit her eyes. She lifted a hand to shield them. A figure in silhouette form was turning towards her down the sloping track.

Oh, it's him again, thought Freya recognising immediately the upright stride of the guy coming towards her.

This morning he was accompanied by two large springer spaniels, both on leads, with his usual silver muzzled black Labrador a few paces behind him, and a much younger cross-breed gambling along ahead.

As they drew level with one another the man looked up, his open face broadening into a smile.

'Beautiful day,' he said.

'Yes,' agreed Freya torn between contemplating his rather shapely legs and meeting his arresting hazel-eyed glance with a smile. 'Absolutely,' she added a second later, congratulating herself on being able to achieve both objectives and speak in such a short space of time.

Neither of them slackened pace as they passed one another.

Ignoring her slightly increased heartbeat, Freya looked round for Henri. Ah, there she was, her nose exploring the interesting bark of a fallen tree, her small stumpy tail wagging for all it was worth.

It really was a wonder the dog walker didn't catch pneumonia thought Freya, the way he walked many and various dogs wearing what looked like old rugby shorts and an equally old sailing jacket in all weathers. Then she wondered why on earth she had even noticed

3

this detail when she had a boyfriend who, apart from being eminently successful at his job, was also drop dead gorgeous, in a way that was immediately apparent to any female with a pulse.

Freya arrived back at her car, noticing the mud bespattered four wheel drive car parked near her. She lifted the boot hatch and encouraged Henri into her dog cage in the back. Nevertheless she was frowning a little as, having settled Henri and changed her shoes and jacket, she drove the few miles to her house in Lyndhurst.

It wasn't that she was unhappy, in any way. She had a good job with a bank in Christchurch; lovely home, although the mortgage was rather higher than she would like; fabulous boyfriend . . .

But, thinking of Jay, Freya's frown intensified. Fabulous. Yes, the word described Jay completely. She remembered the time they'd first met at a friend's party — just catching tantalisingly meagre glimpses of him across a crowded room.

'Who's that fabulous looking bloke

over there?' she'd whispered.

'Oh that'd be Jay,' said Lorna, her friend and work colleague from the bank in Lyndhurst, without even turning her head.

'Jay?'

'Yep. Jay — short for Jason and also fabulously good looking bloke.'

'So — there's a problem?'

'Not that I know of. Just a bit too good to be true, y'know? Everything's been easy for Jason Hamilton. He has a charmed life. Wealthy family, brains, good looks.'

Freya looked back to where Jay was standing, head slightly bent, because he was tall, listening to what a svelte blonde was saying. She had him in profile now.

'Wow,' she said aloud.

'Yes — common reaction . . . '

But Freya was hardly listening because as though feeling her eyes on him, Jay had glanced up, their glances meeting over the blonde's head, and Freya was having difficulty in looking away.

And that had been it really. They'd met and fallen in love and Freya had been introduced to a new world — a world of yachts and Pimms on the terrace. Trips to Cowes, London and Paris. Open top sports cars, bonuses and easy living.

Not that her living had ever been desperately hard. But she'd had to work, had to appreciate the value of money and when she had been left a surprise legacy she had turned it into a deposit for her house.

'You can't go wrong with bricks and mortar,' her father had advised so, even though the payments were higher than she'd have liked, Freya had invested in her small house.

Jay was a high flyer. He worked in investment banking and spent a lot of his time jetting round the world and making deals. Under his influence she'd given up her high ranking, but fairly routine job at the bank in Lyndhurst and taken on another less secure but more lucrative position at a bank in

Christchurch; a branch of the bank Jay worked for in London.

But today Jay was coming to Christchurch. Purely business, he'd said. Thinking of this now and frowning some more, Freya turned the car into her short drive, let Henri out of the car and into her kennelled area, made sure her water bowl was full then, with a glance at her watch locked the back door and set off for work.

The feeling of unease was still with her as she drove. It stemmed back to about a week ago when she'd made some reference to the summer and her plan to have a pond put in the garden. For some reason Jay had changed the subject and when she'd brought it up again in conversation later he'd looked away muttering about goodness knows where anyone would be in a few months' time.

'Well, I know where I'll be,' answered Freya, faint alarm bells ringing. 'I'll be right here digging my pond . . . What about you?'

Jay had shrugged and turned away. But later when they'd kissed goodnight before he'd roared off towards London in his classy car, he'd been as charming and attentive as ever and she'd felt the desire still there within him just as strong as it always had been. So she'd dismissed it. After all, she'd always known he didn't like the idea of being tied down.

He had a flat in London and his own studio apartment over his parent's triple garage in a well-kept and up-market village west of Lyndhurst.

Freya didn't go there much. Somehow she'd never felt comfortable with Jay's glossy, toned and tanned mother, with her tinkling cut glass accent, or his father who was quiet but ineffective in shielding Freya from his wife's more cutting comments.

'Oh, Mum's alright,' said Jay. 'Massive feeling of inadequacy, that's why she likes to show people their place.'

'And what's my place?' asked Freya.

Jay had given a smile that threatened

to stop her heart from beating. 'Right here with me sweetie, right here with me.'

Remembering this now Freya gave herself a mental shake. No, there was nothing wrong. Nothing really wrong anyway. It was just her imagination that was telling her he'd sounded remote on the phone yesterday.

Sometimes she yearned for a little more romance for two in their relationship and maybe a little less of the clever one liners in front of a room full of socialites. A hint of more stability would be good too, she reflected. Jay never seemed to think more than a month ahead.

But all in all she was having a good time and at least Jay was never boring. And their relationship must be pretty serious, mustn't it, for him to have suggested her moving to London? Not that she would. Well, not unless he was really serious and wanted her to get engaged or something like that. Even then she'd have to give it serious thought.

Moving, after all, was a serious thing. But Jay had merely suggested that she sell her house, her most cherished possession for goodness sake; well, after Henri, and buy a studio flat in London so they could see more of one another. Just like that! He didn't seem to realise that she couldn't just do that sort of thing on a mere whim. She'd have to change her job — although he'd implied that he could help there — and totally change her way of living. And what about her family and friends? What about her walks in the New Forest? What about Henri?

Anyway, he obviously hadn't been serious, because he'd never mentioned it again.

Freya had reached the outskirts of Christchurch now. She loved the city, its quay with the splendid priory church behind it. She loved the hustle and bustle of its timeless streets. Yes, she'd made the right decision six months ago in changing her job. No matter what people said about the banking industry, and even her own niggling feelings of doubt when she'd taken her new position, it had been the right thing to do. The work was challenging but she thrived on it.

Humming quietly to herself, she pushed through the swing doors and prepared to meet another day.

★   ★   ★

Harry gave a long, low whistle. The two springers with their liver spotted coats standing out against the green of the spring grass were the first to appear chasing one another towards him.

Blackie, his own faithful friend, momentarily pointed his nose in their direction then looked up at Harry, whose side he never left for long now, with old, wise eyes. It was only the young boxer cross who took more persuasion to come to heel.

Harry whistled again then glanced at his watch. He was behind schedule. By the time he returned the dogs to their owners and arrived back at his own place in the small village of Mindhurst, it would be mid-morning. But it was such a beautiful morning, he reminded himself — and he'd managed a passing 'good morning' with smiling girl, and that, Harry was prepared to admit, made the morning more worthwhile than ever.

In fact, that was the reason he walked the dogs in this particular stretch of forest because, after spotting her several times in the past, he'd realised that she was a creature of habit and made the same walk at more or less the same time every morning. There was absolutely no reason why he shouldn't do the same.

As he'd walked along the well-trodden paths in the area, he'd caught himself rehearsing odd snatches of conversation they might have, should he pluck up the courage. Something other than just good morning. Although 'good morning' was good — of course it was — especially when accompanied by her amazingly attractive smile.

He'd noticed the smile straight away even though at first it had been quite shy and tentative. Then later, when he'd made some small comment regarding ducks and rain, he'd watched the smile broaden into a grin which made her look as though she was enjoying a huge joke. Her grey eyes fringed with dark lashes that matched her dark spiky hair, held a twinkle that looked like fun too.

Yes, she looked like a nice person. A nice, friendly person. The kind of person he'd like to have a long walk with, a conversation with, or even a cup of coffee. More than that he didn't have time for. But, he had to admit that when he parked in his usual forest car parking place, his heart lifted a little if he saw her Mini was already there.

Eventually, Harry made out a speck in the distance which rapidly hurtled towards him. 'Good boy,' said Harry when the powerful body with its over large puppy feet and lolling tongue arrived within calling distance.

He quietened the dog down by speaking calmly then clipped on his lead. 'We've seen smiling girl and you've had your exercise — time to go home boys and girls,' he said heading back in the opposite direction towards the path and car park.

The two springer spaniels went happily enough into their yard at home. They were sisters, both bitches and belonged to a young couple who worked long hours.

The two dogs had an outdoor shed which they used as a daytime kennel and a large yard to run in which Harry had the keys to. He walked them first thing in the morning and at four in the afternoon. They were lovely dogs, worthy of being called show dogs, and Harry kept them on a lead for much of their morning walk in order to strengthen their physique as they strained at the leash.

Butch, the crazy and exciteable young boxer cross was a different kettle of fish altogether. He needed plenty of exercise in order to tire him out and Harry encouraged him to run as much as possible whenever he was in charge of him.

So far he'd proved to be a friendly dog showing little signs of aggression but as he was owned by Jackie, a nervous and somewhat scatty, fifty-year-old widow, Harry kept a close eye on him.

When he reached Jackie's home she was standing at the back door to greet him with a smile of welcome on her face.

Butch jumped up to greet her and Harry couldn't bring himself to tell her she shouldn't encourage him to be so boisterous.

'Thanks Harry,' said Jackie straightening up. 'I'll take him out again myself later. He's always much better behaved if he's been out with you first. He's so strong already, I'm frightened he'll pull me right over.'

'He's a great dog,' said Harry. 'A great character. Good with other dogs and people, too. A little over exuberant maybe, at times, but he's young yet. He'll be fine.'

'Coffee?'

'I won't this time, if you don't mind Jackie. I must get home as I've a lot to do today.'

Harry opened the door of the jeep and climbed in. 'I'll pick Butch up again tomorrow if you like.'

'Please. And thanks a lot Harry.'

He was right; by the time he'd reached the converted or rather half converted barn he called home, most of the morning had gone.

He gave a rueful glance at one of the computers that were lined up on a long desk against the wall. No time to get on with the installation of the shower in the boot-room. At around noon the computers would start buzzing and he'd have to get down to work.

Beautiful morning though, just beautiful.

He put fresh water in the dog bowl and watched as Blackie made his slow arthritic walk across to the tiled kitchen, settled himself on his old checked blanket, then sunk his head on his forepaws and prepared for the serious business of resting.

Harry tidied up a little in the kitchen and put some coffee on.

He registered that the first downloads were taking place on one of his computers. He stretched himself, picked up his coffee mug and sat himself at his work station.

For a moment a vision of smiling girl's face came between him and the computer screen and he found himself wondering what her laugh would sound like if she was really amused.

One of these mornings he might time it exactly right so that he'd finished his walk just as smiling girl started hers. Maybe that way he could find out. Maybe he would be able to make her laugh. Yes, they could exchange a few pleasantries in close proximity to their cars, that way either of them could cut the conversation short and make a quick get-away if need be.

Only he had a very strong feeling he wouldn't be the one to want to make a quick exit. Not at all. He rather thought that against all his better instincts he would like to prolong the acquaintance.

First of all though, there was a job to do. Harry looked at the rows of figures that were scrolling down the screen. Ah, now this looked interesting, very interesting . . .

2

'You don't fancy London then?' Jay said, as he draped a lazy arm round her shoulders.

'What for? A weekend?'

'No. To live . . . I'm serious. We don't see enough of each other. I miss you . . . You could let out your house if you don't want to sell it, and rent a studio-flat in London . . . You wouldn't be out of pocket.' He gave a sudden very attractive grin. 'Come on, you know it makes sense.'

Freya bit down her disbelief. They'd had this discussion before and he knew she didn't like London. Well, not enough to live there. Oh, the capital was certainly exciting with its never silent pulse of life. The wonderful buildings; the romance of the Thames in the evening with a myriad of lights reflected in its waters; the shops full of designer clothes; the museums, art galleries and theatres. Oh yes, she enjoyed London when she visited, but to work there — to live there? Freya didn't think so.

She imagined the hordes of unsmiling strangers spilling out of the underground onto the often dirty streets, the stifling feeling of too many people breathing the same air.

Then, in the social environment, the sensation of being judged for her dress sense and whether or not she was sporting the right handbag. Oh, she understood that not all London's facets could be the same but she was distinctly aware that within Jay's crowd this was the case. She knew enough to realise that she didn't want to be a part of that circle. She'd never fit in and she knew she'd never want to.

'What's brought this on? I don't want to find a new job. I've only been in this one for six months, and I like it. Anyway, what's wrong with the way we are? You have to come here on business, your family live here. We see quite a lot of each other . . . '

'Not enough. It's a drag coming here every time I want to see you.'

'I sometimes come up and see you.'

Even when he was pulling a face Jay still somehow managed to look impossibly handsome.

'And then we have all that hoo-ha ha over the dog.'

'Her name's Henri. And it's my hoo-ha ha, not yours. All you do is click your fingers. It's me who arranges everything and takes her and her things round to Lorna's.'

'Well, there you are. The perfect solution. Can't you give the dog to Lorna on an extended loan?'

'No, I couldn't.' Freya gave a small laugh even though laughing was the last thing she felt like doing. 'She has an awful, dog-intimidating ginger tom, for a start — anyway, what's brought this on all of a sudden?'

'It's not sudden . . . ' He turned away looking slightly sulky. 'It's just, well — I might not be coming down here on business quite so often.'

The half-smile on Freya's lips died. 'What d'you mean?'

'Look, I didn't tell you this, but there's going to be some restructuring at the Christchurch branch. Nothing major . . . '

'Are you losing your job?'

'No! No, nothing like that. Well, I'm not . . . ' He gave a sudden grin. 'You know me. Always land on my feet.'

Never taking her eyes from his face, Freya waited.

He looked away. 'Some will though, no doubt about it. Can't be helped.'

'Let me rephrase that question. Am I losing my job?'

'No! No . . . I'm sure you're not.'

'You're the one who told me to go for this job Jay.'

'I know I did. You're probably safe. Oh, absolutely . . . Bound to be.'

'You don't sound convinced.'

Jay grinned again and stretched out his arm. 'Well, maybe it's time to move

22

on,' he said standing up. 'If it comes to it, and I'm not saying it will . . . Well, you'd get some redundancy.'

Freya stood up too. 'Jay, I've only been there six months. First in, first out. I've got a large mortgage. Any redundancy I was due wouldn't go far.'

'Well, why not do as I suggest? Come to London. You're a bright girl and there's loads of opportunities up there.'

'You don't understand — I've told you before — my life's here.'

Jay turned to face her. 'Well, I never had you down as such a scaredy cat. Your life is wherever you make it happen. You have to make your own opportunities and there's plenty in London.'

'But Jay, I hardly know anyone there . . . ' It sounded pathetic — even to her own ears.

'Yes, I'd noticed that. It's one of the reasons I want you to come to London. And you do know me, don't you? Think of the fun we could have.'

'And what about Henri?'

'What about Henri?' He sounded scornful. 'Don't pass up the opportunity of a lifetime just because of a dog.'

'She's more than just a dog.'

Jay put his finger to his forehead. 'Dah!'

'She's a responsibility — a responsibility I relish,' she said defiantly.

'Well, she's quite a pretty little thing. Pedigree, isn't she? Why don't you sell her? That'd put a bit more money in the pot.'

Freya covered her ears. 'What pot? What are you talking about? One minute we were having a perfectly nice weekend and the next moment you're telling me I've got to change my entire life. Wait a minute, how long have you known about this?'

They were standing facing one another now with a metre between them. 'Don't shout at me,' Jay said, all the humour draining from his face. 'You might have been having a nice weekend. I wasn't, I was having rather a boring weekend actually. No yachting, no parties; all we've done is visit the pub, talk to your friends and walk your pathetic little dog. I don't call that exactly scintillating.'

Ouch, that hurt. Freya opened her mouth. 'I — I thought you liked my friends. I thought you liked me,' she said, feeling the tears in her voice as she spoke.

Jay took a step towards her. 'Of course I like you,' he said. 'I'm crazy about you. My little country girl with your old-fashioned jeans, your spiky hair and your unmade-up face; you're like a breath of fresh air . . . '

He kissed the tip of her nose. 'All I'm saying is — and don't pretend we haven't discussed this before — all I'm saying is — this might be the right time to make the move . . . Now stop scowling at me and get your coat. You can drive me to the Cock Inn and hopefully we'll meet some friends with something interesting to say. Come on, cheer up! I was just warning you about the bank — that's all. It's as well to be aware. But it hasn't happened yet. It most likely never will.'

What am I doing? thought Freya as she obediently fetched her jacket and painted on a smile. We both know it is going to happen, and sooner rather than later.

★　★　★

'Hi Harry, wearing your best again, I see.'

Harry put his pint down on the bar with rather more force than he intended. 'Hello Nadine,' he said, hoping his voice sounded more enthusiastic than he felt.

Sporting a smile that most men would find more than a little seductive, Nadine came towards him.

Her pale marmalade coloured hair looked as though it had only just left the ironing board and it was still carrying a coat of wet spray on varnish; her face was perfectly made up. Her nails were dark red and tapering, almost as though they were dripping with blood. She was dressed from head to toe in cream. Her pale trousers were tucked into chamois high-heeled boots of the palest vanilla, her sweater was of the softest wool — probably cashmere.

Taking care not to touch any part of his sailing jacket that might contaminate her perfection, Nadine leaned over and gave an air kiss to the side of his head. Harry kept his head resolutely still and waited for her to aim another at the other side of his head, aware from experience, that if he moved an iota, she would make it a good excuse to miss aim and manage to touch her lips to his.

'Ah Harry!' she said. 'My little bit of rough. What a sweetie you are. If only I could persuade you to take a shower occasionally we could have such a lovely time together.'

And just how was Harry supposed to answer that? Particularly when her absent husband was one of his best friends. Harry gave a reserved smile and looked round wildly for rescue. But the only other inhabitants of The Speckled Hen were two teenagers who hardly looked old enough to be drinking and a couple of old country boys who stared at Nadine as though she had just escaped from the pages of *Hello*.

The landlord edged his way towards her. 'Gin and tonic,' said Nadine briefly. She fished in her cream leather bag for a purse. 'It's alright Harry, I need some change.'

'I only came in for a quick one, Nadine,' volunteered Harry with an eye on the door.

A glass and bottle of tonic water were placed at her elbow by the unsmiling landlord.

After contemplating the glass for a moment as though there might be something not quite perfect about it, Nadine silently passed a twenty pound note across the bar's highly polished surface. She used the same red taloned hand to push a strand of pale hair from her forehead. 'I was hoping you'd take pity on me, Harry. Keep me company for a bit. It gets so lonely when Nick's abroad.'

'Well, wish I could,' lied Harry. 'But you know how it is. Dogs and work. Dogs and work. Occasional foray to the pub and that's it.' He gave a self-deprecating smile. 'Story of my life I'm afraid.'

'We could change that Harry.'

How Harry hated this clever kind of half serious chatting up. Especially when it came from the wife of his friend. He tossed off what he hoped was an amused chuckle. 'Just as well I'm a great friend of Nick's,' he said.

'Nick's not here,' purred Nadine.

'That doesn't mean he's not still a great friend of mine,' replied Harry as he finished his drink.

'Silly, I was only kidding.'

Yes, sure you were, thought Harry.

Aloud he said, 'I know you were Nadine.'

'Wait Harry, I was going to ask you if

you'd take Za Za, when you walk the other dogs this afternoon. I'd really appreciate it,' she simpered.

'Sorry Nadine. No can do. I'm taking four at the moment including Blackie. Only two cages in the back of the wagon. Besides Za Za's such a little thing, she'd never keep up.'

'I thought Blackie was dead by now — he must be a hundred years old!'

'No,' said Harry coldly. 'He's very much alive I can assure you.'

'Anyway, Za Za wouldn't take up much room,' wheedled Nadine. 'And she'd keep up — she has lots of pent up energy for such a small dog. Bichon Frise need plenty of exercise or they get fat . . . '

'But you take her out, don't you? How do you get your exercise?' Bad question Harry — you walked right into that one.

But for once Nadine missed out on a potential for innuendo. 'Oh, I go to the gym.'

Of course, what else?

'Well, a dog's not just for Christmas, or a fashion accessory,' said Harry sternly. 'You've got to look after her.'

'How can you say that? I'm devoted to her, but I think she needs the company of other dogs.'

Harry looked at her suspiciously. Nadine worrying about her dog's mental welfare? It didn't quite ring true somehow.

'Please Harry,' said Nadine in a put on little girl voice which irritated him almost beyond endurance.

'I'll let you know if I get a vacancy,' promised Harry, intending no such thing but anxious to terminate the conversation. 'Have to go now. Work pressing — you know how it is.' Quickly, he stood up. 'See you Saul,' he called to the barman before making for the door.

'Cheers Harry,' answered the barman.

'I'd like more ice in this,' said Nadine regarding Saul with a superior expression. 'And another slice of lemon.'

★ ★ ★

31

Harry let himself back into the barn. Although he had facilities in the yard to kennel at least six dogs, he had none boarding at present. In the summer he thought he'd probably have a few though.

He had never advertised. In fact the whole dog walking business had come about by accident really.

It started with him doing a favour for Saul the landlord of The Speckled Hen, who had asked him to help with his dogs while he recovered from an operation. Although Harry had been quite prepared to walk the two old dogs along with Blackie as a favour, Saul had insisted on paying him and somehow word had got around Mindhurst that if you needed someone to walk your dog — Harry was your man.

Harry didn't mind. It did him good, he reckoned, to get out regularly and stretch his legs.

His desk job, albeit mainly managed from home, involved a great deal of figure and computer work and it was too easy to become so engrossed he didn't notice the time passing. Being cooped up all day with no exercise was a habit that Harry, a country boy at heart, had no desire to get into. So early every morning he took whichever dogs were on his list at the time, out for a long walk in the forest and then at about four in the afternoon went out again for a shorter run this time along the paths at the edge of the village.

No, on the whole, Harry didn't mind anything much. He was a fairly laid back character most of the time and his way of life suited him.

He'd had a taste of another sort of life before where clockwatching and wearing an expensive suit had been the order of the day. When dashing from one airport to another, from one hotel room to the next, never being quite certain which time zone he was in or which client he would have to charm or assess had been a way of life — a lifestyle of which he had suddenly become heartily sick.

In contrast the life he was living now was like a spell in heaven.

The project of the barn was on-going but not urgent. His work with the American bank was enough to keep his brain active and the wolf from the door and, on top of this, he had calm, peace and quiet and close proximity to nature.

Yes, he was a lucky man.

Now, if only he could get smiling girl to do more than just smile at him — say a few words perhaps. Well, life would be very sweet indeed.

3

Unlike many of her fellow workers, Freya didn't usually mind Mondays. She liked routine. Liked to get up in the morning, shower and dress for the office — all apart from her footwear because of course, she always took Henri for her walk first thing. Mostly she wore trainers or boots dependant on the weather, then changed them before she went to work.

Freya loved that early morning walk. She enjoyed feeling the first cool rush of fresh air on her skin, watching the enthusiasm of Henri's cute furry rump wiggling backwards and forwards in an effort to keep up with her tail as she preceded Freya towards the car.

It had been raining the night before so today Freya had carefully tucked her tailored black trousers into her waterproof boots. After a glance at the sky, she'd also pulled on her old wax jacket. She put the car into gear and made her usual right turn out of her driveway.

Oh yes, today was Monday, but for once Freya felt uneasy about going into the office. How could she feel comfortable knowing that at any moment the axe might fall and that she and many others could be out of a job?

Well, you asked the question, she reminded herself. Many times since she'd wished she hadn't, but still a small part of her was glad that she had because at least she knew where she stood now. Or rather didn't stand, because, of course being the last one in she didn't really have any standing at all, did she? Added to that was the fact her current position was in middle management — a dangerous place to be. Oh, why had she taken on such an absurdly high mortgage? And why had she taken Jay's advice six months ago and changed her job?

But perhaps Jay was right and it was time she broke free from her old roots.

Perhaps meeting him then changing her job was all part of her life plan. Maybe the next logical step was to move to London, find a place quite close to where he lived — she didn't want to crowd him — then just see how things panned out. It couldn't be fair, could it, really, to expect Jay to carry on a relationship round weekends only?

But what about Henri?

For the moment she pushed that thought aside and concentrated on human relationships. It hadn't seemed to matter at first that Jay was a city person and she a country girl through and through. In fact, she supposed that the difference between them had been part of the attraction. Added to his male model good looks, his way of looking to her as though she was the only girl in the world and the way — well, they'd just clicked. But if she went to London, what about Henri?

There she was again, thinking about her dog first.

She gave a sigh. Anyway, it was no

good her dawdling along like this, she'd just have to wait and see what this week brought. Worrying about what decision to make before she was even faced with the choices wouldn't really help.

Out of habit, Freya glanced at her watch as she pulled into her usual car park in the forest's clearing. She was later than usual and found that for once, the dog walker had beaten her — his mud bespattered jeep was already parked some twenty yards away.

Neatly pulling into her customary spot she observed the dog walker bent over at the back of his vehicle. He was probably fixing the dogs' leads. Freya got out of her Mini and opened Henri's cage. Like a shot Henri jumped to the ground and hared over to the old black Labrador that was sitting patiently watching his master.

Henri splashed through two very large puddles. Oh no, she was going to jump all over the dog walker covering his bare legs with mud in the process.

'Henri sit!' screamed a hot-faced Freya.

The dog walker looked round in surprise, saw her, grinned and promptly sat down next to the large dog cage on the tailgate of his vehicle.

Henri lost interest in him and as an alternative sniffed at the two springer spaniels; then, before Freya had the wits to call her, she joyfully bounded off with what looked like a teenage delinquent boxer cross in close pursuit.

'I'm so sorry,' panted Freya having sprinted across the car park. 'She's usually quite obedient.'

'More than can be said of Butch — he's a raving lunatic. Not dangerous you understand, just full of energy.'

'Henri usually sits on command,' went on Freya, trying hard not to look at his strong legs which were definitely worth looking at, and finding herself turning her attention to his mouth instead which was stretched into a very attractive grin.

'Well, let me congratulate you on your style of dog training at least. That was a very authoritative command — I obeyed immediately.'

Freya wrinkled her nose and smiled.

'My name,' he said standing up and holding out his free hand, 'happens to be Henry.'

Freya smiled. 'No!'

'Well, strictly speaking — yes, but I'm always called Harry . . . Quite took me back to my school days. One very memorable teacher by the name of Miss Wilkes always called me Henry. For a moment I thought she was right here in the middle of the New Forest reprimanding me for some terrible transgression.' He laughed again.

'Sorry,' said Freya, laughing more than was strictly necessary. Then, because she didn't really want to end the conversation with this handsome man, she added, 'Are all these dogs yours?'

'No, only the well behaved one.' He indicated the black Lab. 'His name's Blackie. He's very old, and a bit deaf and arthritic but otherwise in good health. These others I walk for friends in my village . . . I might as well walk four as one.'

Freya bent down and fondled Blackie's ears. 'Hello old boy, you're lovely, aren't you? Good boy, good boy . . . I'd better go and find Henri,' she went on, straightening up again.

'Oh, one thing I should point out . . . '

'Yes?' She was already negotiating the puddles on her way back to lock her car and glanced back at him over her shoulder.

'Your 'dog' is actually a bitch.'

'Yes, I know.'

'So why have you given her a bloke's name?'

Freya shrugged and smiled some more. 'I spell it with an 'i' — makes it more feminine.'

'Your dog can read?'

Freya laughed. 'I thought it was cute — that's all.'

'Ah, cute — that'd do it,' he said grinning.

So the dog walker didn't only have nice legs, he also had a sense of humour. But somehow she'd known that anyway — hadn't she? She'd just known he'd be nice. Freya locked the car and looked round for Henri, who by now had panicked and came hurtling back towards her.

'Good girl,' she said automatically fondling the little dog's coat. Casually she glanced over to the group of dogs by the four wheel drive.

Oh no, oh yes, Harry was waiting for her. The springer spaniels were straining at their leashes, Butch was dancing round in circles with his tongue hanging out and Blackie was waiting with an expression of pained resignation in his eyes.

'Hi,' she said when she drew level. 'My name's Freya. I've seen you here before. D'you come here every morning?'

'Pretty much,' answered Harry. 'The dogs love it. There's wooded areas and open spaces. I can see them most of the time, yet they can have a good run. Also it's not too far away from Mindhurst where I live.'

'Mindhurst?'

'Yes. D'you know it?'

'I've driven through it now and then. There's some nice old buildings there — and a very quaint country pub if I'm not mistaken,' she added.

'Ah yes. The Speckled Hen, I know it well.'

'Good reputation for food.'

'That's right. The beer's excellent too.'

Freya found that almost without realising it they had fallen into step. The two younger dogs, Henri and Butch, were running wildly in all directions, the spaniels were straining at their leashes and Blackie was keeping up with them quite sedately at the rear.

She asked why he was keeping the springers on leashes and he explained to her about building muscle and strength.

As he expounded it soon became apparent that there wasn't much Harry didn't know about dogs.

'Hope I'm not boring you,' he said. 'I've always loved dogs, ever since I was a kid. Especially Labs. They're so faithful, y'know? My dad had a curly haired chocolate Lab once. That dog would have gone through fire, crossed a raging river for my dad . . . Not too many humans you'd get that kind of devotion from.'

They walked in a comfortable silence for a while.

Freya sneaked a sideways glance at him. He had a good, strong profile. Not good-looking exactly. Maybe his nose was a little crooked at the tip and his face was a little too craggy to be considered conventionally handsome, but there was something very kind in his expression and the lines of humour round his mouth made him appear friendly and approachable.

They cut through the woods and came out to the heath-like area where she'd often seen him in the past.

'I just love this bit,' she gushed before she could stop herself. 'It's especially good this time of year with everything so fresh, but even in winter it looks great.'

They slowed to a halt. 'Yep,' said

Harry. 'Timeless, isn't it? I bet if you went back a couple of centuries it would still look the same. The same types of trees and animals, the same contours to the land, the same wild ponies, although maybe more of them. Yep, it's pretty perfect I'd say in spring . . . Although when the gorse comes out and the heathland's baked dry from the sun — it still looks great then.'

'Autumn's a good time too,' said Freya thinking that they were beginning to sound like a nature program. 'The colours sometimes are just so rich what with the purple heather and the trees turning . . . It's really hard to choose a best time, isn't it?'

Harry whistled for Butch, who turned his nose in acknowledgement but never slackened speed as he reached the brow of the incline. Henri paused, obviously torn for a moment between following her new-found friend and rushing back to check on Freya.

'Don't worry, he'll be back in a moment, he's just trying it on.'

'Have you lived in this area for long?' asked Freya, keeping up with him even though the ground was rougher and she had to watch where she was placing her feet.

'Look out, that bit's boggy. Don't splash your trousers. You look like you're ready for work.'

'You're right — shouldn't wear them really but I never seem to have time to change when I get back.'

'That's why I wear shorts,' said Harry. 'To avoid changing jeans three times a day . . . Anyway, in answer to your question, no, I haven't actually lived in Hampshire long but I have friends here. I came here a lot as a kid. We used to come on camping holidays and I always loved it . . . You?'

'Born and bred,' said Freya smiling. 'Lyndhurst to be precise. I live on the outskirts now. I know the whole area pretty well. Well, I would, wouldn't I, having lived here all my life? The forest was originally a royal hunting preserve for William the Conqueror. You don't get much older than that. His treasury was at Winchester.'

Harry grinned. 'Really?'

Freya grinned back. 'Yes, really.'

'You wouldn't happen to be a teacher?'

'Not a chance, and I'm not related to your Miss Wilkes either. No, I work in a bank in Christchurch,' she pulled a face, 'hence the smart trousers. Good girl Henri,' she added as the small panting dog arrived back at her heels, looking up at her with adoring eyes. 'She wants a treat for coming back,' she said to Harry.

Harry was scanning the horizon. 'Come on Butch,' he said. 'You've been out of sight long enough . . . Excuse me Freya, I'm going to have to go after him . . . He's such a pain . . . Oh no, there he is — I warn you, he'll be covered in mud if not worse, and smell disgusting. Don't let him rub up against you whatever you do.'

Freya looked at her watch. 'I'm going to have to turn back anyway, I have to take Henri home then get to Christchurch for work.'

Harry turned towards her. She'd been right, his smile really was most attractive. His eyes twinkled with warmth and his expression changed from open but fairly ordinary to well, really quite something.

'Ah, well,' he started. 'It was really nice talking to you . . . Um, you know the pub we were talking about — The Speckled Hen?'

Oh dear, now she didn't know quite where to look. She gave a nod.

'Well, I was thinking maybe we might meet up there sometime . . . Just for a beer . . . '

'Um yes, that would be nice . . . But um, I do have a boyfriend — so better not, eh.'

For a brief moment disappointment showed, sharp and clear in his hazel eyes. Then he gave a half laugh. 'Yes, of course you do. Not to worry. Might bump into you another time . . . Dog walking . . . ' He turned away — then back again, pulling on the springers' leads. 'What's your boyfriend's name?'

'Sorry,' said Freya finding that she was really, very sorry. 'His name's Jay. Jay Hamilton.'

'Jay. Well, tell Jay he's a lucky bloke . . . Bye Freya . . . Come on Blackie, keep up, you can do it.'

'Bye Harry,' Freya said quietly before turning and walking rather quickly in the opposite direction.

★   ★   ★

Well, Harry, just what did you expect? he thought to himself as he continued the walk. Pretty girl like that. Not only pretty, but smart and also quite sweet. Loved the countryside, loved dogs, friendly nature and with the sunniest smile.

What a fool to have even asked the question, what an idiot. Boyfriend? With a smile like that of course she had a boyfriend. You idiot Harry.

She had a boyfriend. A boyfriend

called Jay. Harry's lip curled. He should have asked if the boyfriend's surname was Walker — then it would be jay-walker as opposed to dog-walker. No, that wouldn't have been very funny. Pathetic more like. She might not be the kind of girl to appreciate a pun at her boy-friend's expense.

So it was goodbye smiling girl. Well, goodbye Freya actually — at least he knew that now. Pretty name — it suited her.

They'd been getting on so well too. Conversation had been easy with none of those awkward gaps that sometimes appeared when first you got to know someone. No, nothing like that.

Ah well, forget it. Just forget it. But that smile. Harry knew the smile would take some forgetting.

4

The axe had fallen a week later. The banks, it was explained, were tidying up their acts. They were all tightening their belts and cutting out dead wood. Freya wasn't sure she liked being compared to an old tree branch, but, however it was put, the message was the same. She'd been given an interview with 'human resources', another term she wasn't fond of, at the end of which — despite the sympathy and promise of good references — she'd been told to clear her desk.

Although by nature Freya was an optimist, after scanning her computer for suitable jobs in the area and in her line, and finding none, she was beginning to feel very despondent.

Jay had been surprisingly supportive, though she couldn't help feeling that it was to be expected considering that he was the one who'd encouraged her to go for the job in Christchurch. He told her there were still good jobs going in the city and that she could stay with him until she got a place sorted out.

Somehow that wasn't quite what she wanted to hear.

'Why on earth not?' asked her friend Lorna who was still safely employed at the bank in Lyndhurst. 'You could rent out your house — no trouble at this time of year — either as holiday lets or on a six month lease. Why not? See how it pans out.' She gave a sudden grin. 'And you never know, if you move in with Jay you might not want to move out again.'

'Whoa!' said Freya. 'I'm an independent girl, I'm not moving in with anyone until I'm good and ready. I don't really want to live in London and anyway — what about Henri? You have to have a garden if you have a dog and I just know she'd hate London . . . No, I'm going to have to put the house up for rent, I know that, because if I sell, it will be at a loss. I'll have to find a cheap, ground floor flat with a garden and some kind of a job — any old job will do. Maybe a seasonal job, at a garden centre or something, just so I can afford to live until things get better again.'

'Well, if you really get stuck,' said Lorna, 'you can move in with us for a little while.'

Freya eyed her friend for a long moment. 'Okay then, I'll come tomorrow,' she said straight faced, then burst out laughing at the expression on Lorna's face.

'Sorry,' she said when she'd recovered. 'I take it you haven't yet mentioned this to Mike? No, I somehow didn't think so. No, I appreciate the offer but I'll find something — I have to.'

But, it was easier said than done. Although letting the house on a six month lease was surprisingly simple, finding a cheap flat with a garden suitable for herself and Henri was not.

'Bad time of year,' said one estate agent after another. 'People feeling the credit crunch are doing what you're doing — renting out their own properties as holiday lets — all the smaller flats have gone.'

Freya began to lose heart.

'What are we going to do?' she said despondently to Henri on one of their early morning walks. 'My tenants are due to move in at the end of the month and I've got nowhere apart from that miserable little bed-sit that doesn't allow dogs.'

But Henri wasn't interested, she'd picked up a familiar scent and with her nose down was busy following it. With a joyous bark she disappeared down a woodland path that Freya rarely took because it consisted in the main of muddy puddles that never seemed to dry out.

'Oh, alright then,' said Freya. After all who was there to care whether or not her jeans were filthy? She wouldn't be seeing Jay until mid-week when, against her better instincts, she was travelling to London for a couple of days. She was not looking forward to the meeting which she'd agreed to in a weak moment.

'Honestly Freya, how can you be so dismissive of London and all it has to offer when you haven't even tried looking for a job?' Jay had said in his most persuasive tone. 'Let me line up a few options for you — please.'

Well, it would have been churlish to refuse — wouldn't it? And now he'd phoned and said she'd got two interviews to go to over Tuesday and Wednesday of next week so fait accompli — she had to go, didn't she? No choice in the matter. She wondered how he'd be if she managed to swing an interview and still refused to make the decision to move to London.

Frowning slightly Freya ducked under a couple of overhanging branches and followed Henri into the dimness of the woodland path. It proved to be just as hazardous as she'd expected. Avoiding the deepest depressions, Freya kept to the edges. Henri had long since disappeared.

There were some ominous crashing noises just round the bend of the path. Expecting a wild boar at worst or a Great Dane at the very least, Freya pressed herself up against the woodland verge.

Then just as Butch hurtled around the corner into sight she heard a shout. 'Butch — here boy — here!'

A bounding Butch, followed closely by his shadow Henri, launched himself at Freya, his pink tongue lolling towards her unsuspecting cheek.

'Down boy,' ordered Freya.

With an expression of complete surprise on his face, Butch complied.

'I'm impressed,' said an amused voice that Freya had no difficulty in recognising as Harry's.

'Just a knack I have,' said Freya, laughing, never taking her eyes off Butch who was sitting obediently on the path and staring back at her as though mesmerised.

Harry slipped a lead onto Butch's collar. 'He's been playing up all morning . . . He's forfeited his freedom for the moment I'm afraid.'

'Where are the others?' asked Freya looking round for the springers. Harry straightened up and their glances met. He had hazel eyes Freya noticed, with a hint of amusement in their depths. He gave a grin and the amusement turned to a warmth she couldn't help but respond to.

'It's Saturday. I don't take them out on a Saturday. They're with their owners somewhere, just as Butch should be — if he wasn't such a maniac.'

Of course it was Saturday. All the days seemed to merge into one another since she'd given up work, or rather since work had given her up.

'I forgot it was Saturday,' she said.

'Oh? But you're later than usual — surely?'

'Yep,' said Freya on a sudden impulse to confide. 'I've been made redundant from the bank so Henri's been getting her exercise a bit later in the day recently.'

'Oh dear,' said Harry sympathetically. 'I know what that feels like! Happened to me over a year ago now. You feel like you've been flung on the scrap heap, don't you?'

'Yes, that's exactly what it feels like, but there are other complications.'

'Oh dear,' said Harry again.

They'd been walking single file in order to avoid the muddy patches but now the path widened out into a clearing. Blackie was sitting patiently by a fallen log. He turned his head at the sound of Harry's quiet 'Good boy.'

Freya walked over and put a hand out to scratch the back of Blackie's head. 'Hello old fellow,' she said. 'You're such a sweet, patient dog.'

'He is,' agreed Harry sitting down on the log. 'His arthritis is playing him up a bit at the moment. I'm hoping the better weather will improve it . . . He can't walk as far as he used to, poor old boy.' He let Butch off his lead again and watched the young dog as he sniffed his way across the clearing with Henri following not too far behind.

As the sun briefly emerged from behind a cloud Freya turned her face towards it feeling more at peace than she had for a long time — sitting here silently with Harry, surrounded by nature and a few dogs. If only life could be like this always.

'You mentioned other complications? Anything you'd like to talk about?'

Freya heaved a sigh. 'My mortgage is colossal so I've had to let my house out,' she said.

'Bit soon for that, isn't it?'

'Well no, I'm the sole owner you see and I really don't want to get behind with the mortgage. None of the banks in the area are looking for staff . . . Well, obviously I will get another job, I'm young and capable, but it'll probably be seasonal and won't pay so well.'

'What about your boyfriend?'

'Jay? Oh, he wants me to go to

London — that's where he's based. He says he'll help me get a job there.'

Harry looked away. 'Sounds an ideal solution.'

'I know, but I don't want to. I don't want to go to London. I want to stay here. This is my home . . . Besides there's Henri . . . '

And Jay doesn't really like dogs thought Freya with sudden clarity. Well, that wasn't exactly fair. He didn't exactly dislike dogs, so long as they were someone else's responsibility, but she had the feeling that if all else failed he wouldn't have the least compunction in taking Henri to the vet. She squashed the thought as rapidly as it had occurred, but all the same it left her with an unpleasant feeling.

There was silence for a couple more minutes.

'So, what are you thinking of doing?'

She looked up with a smile. 'I'm looking for a ground floor flat with a garden, but — well, so far the only thing I can afford is a crummy bed-sit with no facilities for dogs, so — don't know really.'

Harry said nothing.

'Anyway,' said Freya suddenly standing up. 'It's much too nice to sit here feeling sorry for myself. I promised Henri a really long walk this morning — at least that doesn't cost anything.'

'Mind if we tag along with you for a while?' asked Harry. 'We're working our way in a circle back to the car park, so we'll leave you at the top of the rise over there.'

'Fine,' said Freya, thinking for a moment that it was fine and that even though he'd said absolutely nothing that was of any help whatsoever, just being with Harry had made her feel better.

* * *

Harry shortened his stride to fit with Freya's; Blackie ambled slowly at his master's heels.

It was impossible to describe even to

himself just how he'd felt when he'd seen Freya standing on the woodland path, with her dark spiky hair and her ready smile. Impossible to explain the glow that had started within him just at the mere sight of her.

It was good that they had the dogs for distraction or he might have made a fool of himself by staring at her like a moonstruck idiot. Of course it was awful that she'd lost her job, not good at all, but on the other hand it seemed that 'the boyfriend' had been unable to persuade her to move to London, that surely must be welcome news.

Perhaps the relationship wasn't quite as strong as he'd feared. For a moment he almost felt like humming.

He watched the little spaniel prancing at Freya's heels. How could he see her again? If she wasn't walking her dog at regular times any more, how on earth was he to ensure that their paths crossed — because if there was one thing he was very sure of it was that he very much did want their paths to cross again.

They were approaching the top of the rise now. Any moment and she would disappear. Harry racked his brains for anything he could do to delay the moment that would prevent that happening.

'Look,' he said. 'This might not be appropriate, but I'm living in an old barn I'm slowly converting. There are only a few parts that I would call even vaguely habitable, but outside there are a couple of old stables and a secure yard. I often board dogs when their owners are away. Only people I know or know of . . . So, if you're really stuck where Henri is concerned, I could have her — so long as she doesn't have any complicated dietary requirements. You could come and take her out whenever you like.'

Freya stopped walking and turned to face him, her grey eyes huge in her face. Harry's heart beat a little faster.

'Oh Harry,' she started and his heart-beat progressed from a trot to a canter. 'That's really kind of you but well, I couldn't bear to be parted from her.

Anyway I doubt I could afford it . . . '

Harry felt his face flush. 'I wasn't thinking of charging. Well,' he went on hurriedly seeing her expression tighten, 'you could pay for her food if you like. But I'm sure she'd be no bother . . . ' His voice tailed off because Freya's eyes were still saying — thanks, but no thanks.

'Okay, we'll think about it. It's really sweet of you, Harry, but I'm sure I'll find something.'

She looked very small and vulnerable standing there next to him on the brow of the hill. The collar of her wax jacket was up making her neck appear fragile and pale and her spiky hair ruffled slightly in a sudden breeze.

Harry felt a sudden urge to put a brotherly arm round her and give her a hug. For a mad moment he felt his arm move towards her. In panic he directed it instead to shield his eyes and gave a quite unnecessary shout for Butch who was already bounding towards him.

'Well, goodbye then,' said Freya

looking all the same as though she was quite sorry that this was the parting of their ways.

'Look,' said Harry fishing in his wallet for a card, 'I don't like to think of you in a fix. Take my card and ring me if there's anything I can do to help. Looking after Henri would be fine — I look after dogs for people all the time — it's not a commercial business, it's just something I do.' He held out the card and nearly gave a whoop of joy as Freya's fingers closed over it.

'Thanks Harry, you've been really — um — kind.' She put the card in her pocket without looking at it. 'See you around maybe.' She let her hand stray over Blackie's smooth head. 'Bye Blackie.'

Harry stood staring after her until she and her frisky little dog disappeared from sight.

5

Freya sat on board the southward bound train feeling relieved and relaxed for the first time in forty eight hours. It was Thursday and she was on her way home.

Not that she hadn't had a good time. She had, she assured herself, had an amazing time. Jay had met her at the station looking so incredibly handsome and impressive in a pin-striped shirt and charcoal grey suit that she'd felt almost scared of him.

They'd gone on to dinner at a small chic restaurant and eaten remarkably simple food served in an incredibly complicated manner. The waiter appeared to know Jay well and treated Freya as though she was made of porcelain, taking her chain store jacket with hardly a glance at the label and stowing her rather battered weekend bag without a blink.

Over dinner Jay had briefed her on her first interview which was with a pensions company. 'It's not top notch, and I know you're capable of more, but it will give you an 'in' and that's the important thing,' said Jay. 'I've already given them your CV and they're impressed, and of course my recommendation helps,' he added with the smile that usually made Freya go weak at the knees, but this time somehow didn't.

The next morning she attended the interview. The office seemed very plush, the staff glossy and the job, well, frankly — boring. But that wouldn't matter. Beggars, as she well knew, could not be choosers. Her interview had finished by lunchtime. Freya joined a queue of office smart crowds on the pavements. Yes, there certainly was a buzz here in the city. Everyone looked impressively busy. If they weren't engaged in animated conversation, they were flicking through notes taken from their briefcases or operating their mobiles. Everyone looked very — important.

Could it be fun — a worthwhile experience — to work here, to live here, with theatres and art galleries on your doorstep? After all, as Jay kept reminding her, if she felt too hemmed in there were always the parks to take solace in.

But what about Henri? What about Lorna and Mike and all her other friends? What about the friendly country pubs, Mrs P in her local post office; the wonderful open spaces, the beaches, the laziness of having nothing pressing to do? What about her life?

'You really are an old stick in the mud,' said Jay, when she voiced these thoughts later. 'Where's your sense of adventure? You're twenty-five not sixty-five. If you weren't so pretty,' he added with a smile, 'I'd stop bothering with you.' *Would he really?* thought Freya, and found she didn't want to dwell on that question for too long.

The second interview hadn't gone so well. It had been with a large financial company. The computer system was one with which Freya was familiar and the salary they were offering was good, but she didn't take to the head of department who was interviewing her, or the woman from Human Resources who was sitting in. It felt like a cold, impersonal work space. But it was still a job, she argued with herself, and she was very lucky to be considered on Jay's say so.

That evening they met some of Jay's friends for drinks. The venue was smart, the drinks were chilled, the company and dialogue fast and — so smattered with 'in' jokes and references to people she'd never heard of — largely indecipherable. Freya sat on the edge of the conversation toying with a long stemmed glass of wine and wishing herself back in Lyndhurst with her own friends.

'You okay?' asked Jay carelessly, looking across at her at one point.

'Fine,' answered Freya feeling anything but. Then she straightened her shoulders and smiled at a guy who looked younger than her, and slightly shy, and found herself talking to him and trying to put him at ease.

'Nice crowd, aren't they?' said Jay sleepily when they got back to his flat. 'You'd soon fit in . . . Get yourself a new wardrobe and maybe a new haircut — spiky is a bit yesterday . . . You'll pass for a London girl in no time.'

Freya couldn't trust herself to reply.

'By the way, it was good of you to bother with Robin, but you needn't have put yourself out. He's only the equivalent of an office junior you know. No one important.'

'I was an office junior once,' replied Freya.

Jay gave a laugh. 'That's what I miss about you Freya — you're just so nice. Now come here and let me kiss you.'

And she had.

And now she was glad to be on the train and on her way back to civilisation. But not glad to be feeling so confused.

The problem was there was a London Jay and a New Forest Jay. When Jay came to the country, he seemed like a foreign, exotic, creature; maybe a shade too rich for everyday living, but fascinating, glamorous and totally irresistible. When in London, apart from feeling like a fish out of water herself, Freya wasn't sure about the city Jay. There was a predatory air about him, a slick confidence and a way of saying 'Yah — can do' every five seconds which, if she allowed herself to think about it, sorely grated.

They'd parted in a rush. He had to get into work for a meeting which was naturally very important, and Freya — well Freya just wanted to get home.

'I'll see you at the weekend,' Jay said as he left the flat. 'Friday night — I'll text you.'

'Well, I've got packing to do. I know I'm letting it furnished but I'll have to put stuff in storage soon.'

'Sure, sure. Whatever. I'll text you,' he said again kissing her forehead. 'We'll have a good talk over the weekend while you're packing — promise.'

And he'd gone, and Freya had sighed with relief.

Yes, there was a London Jay and a country Jay, just as there was a London Freya and a country Freya. Trouble was she only seemed to like the country versions of both of them. She watched the grey, built-up areas that were speeding by, gradually change to a more rural landscape and pondered the thought.

★　★　★

Lorna met her at the station as arranged. When Henri was let out of the back of the car she promptly produced a puddle with the excitement at seeing Freya again.

'Enjoy yourself?'

'Yes, but it's nice to be home,' answered Freya fending off Henri's frenzied kisses.

'Any luck on the job front?'

'Only the two interviews, and I'm not bursting with anticipation. Jobs were fairly mundane really, not much responsibility. If I was lucky enough to get one it would be a starting point, that's all.'

They got into the car and drove off.

'Jay alright?'

'Yep.'

'Any more you want to tell me?'

'Nope.'

'Does that mean we are no longer looking for a ground floor flat with a dog-proof garden?'

'No it doesn't. It means I'm looking twice as hard . . . How was Henri?'

'Oh, Henri was alright.' Lorna looked at her sideways. 'I had trouble convincing Rufus she wasn't some kind of new treat for cats though.'

'He's a thug. You managed to keep them apart then?'

'Just about. No, it was okay. But you know what cats are like, especially ginger toms. They're spiteful. I had to keep them apart, or poor Henri would have been scratched to pieces.'

Henri chose that moment to give a pathetic whimper.

'She knows we're talking about her.'

'Wouldn't surprise me in the least,' said Lorna navigating the small lanes with dexterity. 'So you still haven't made up your mind then? These two days didn't do it?'

Freya bit her lip. 'I'm hopeless, aren't I? I just don't want to be forced into a decision I feel I'm not ready to make. I never was one to believe in fate and all that. I've known Jay a while but most of the time he's in London. I was thinking about it on the train — I feel as though I only really see the New Forest Jay and when I do see the London Jay he's — oh, I don't know — he's just different.'

Freya looked out of the window at the passing countryside that she loved so much. 'Anyway, I don't want to talk about it any more. I'll spend the next couple of days on a serious house hunt, and in packing up what I can. I don't think . . . I really don't think I'll be going to London.'

'When are you seeing Jay again?'

'He's coming at the weekend — it's his mother's birthday.'

'What will you tell him?'

'I don't know,' answered Freya honestly.

★ ★ ★

It was Saturday again. Harry had got up with hope in his heart and taken Blackie and Butch with him for their usual walk. And had he accidentally on purpose met up with Freya this morning? No, he had not. And he was most definitely disappointed.

The week had crawled by. He'd walked the dogs religiously, looking out all the while for a spiky-haired silhouette that might be Freya. When she hadn't appeared on any of the weekday mornings he'd set his heart on Saturday; he even started out at the same time as last week and trodden the same path.

No Freya.

No phone call either regarding the dog boarding offer he'd made, or anything else for that matter. He'd now reluctantly come to the conclusion that the writing on the wall was saying Freya and Harry were just not meant to be. It was goodbye to smiling girl.

But he was still concerned. He

wondered whether she'd had to give up ownership of her dog, which he was sure would break her heart.

No matter how many times he told himself it was none of his business, he kept remembering her face as she'd said she couldn't bear to be parted from Henri; recalling the way her voice had trembled a little and, because he'd been watching so closely, he'd noticed a minute quivering of her lip. He also recollected how very much he'd wanted to wrap his arms round her and give her a hug.

But Freya had a boyfriend, even if at a distance. Freya would be fine. The best thing he could do was stop thinking about her and get on with his life.

Even so he stayed out longer than he'd intended, half hoping that Freya would make a miraculous appearance. Eventually he took Butch back to Jackie and suggested that as there'd been a marked improvement in his behaviour this week, he was just about ready for obedience classes.

Later, back at the barn, he rather half-heartedly set about fixing a shower in the corner of the boot-room. The plumbing was already installed and because the boot-room had a convenient drain in the corner and was tiled throughout, it was a relatively simple job, but one that he'd been putting off.

Despite his initial lack of enthusiasm, by one thirty he'd more or less completed the task and was berating himself for not attempting it in the earlier winter months when hosing down muddy dogs was a daily chore.

Crikey, he thought looking round, what with the heat from the old wood-burner in the main area next door filtering through, a person could very nearly live in this add-on boot-room and cloakroom as a self-contained unit. Shame really — he had to drag himself all the way to the other end of the barn for the makeshift kitchen, decrepit bathroom and miniscule bedroom.

Well, the bathroom wasn't decrepit exactly, just functional and somewhat lacking in style, but the kitchen, which consisted of an old table, an even older dresser, a fridge and an ageing free-standing electric cooker, he had to admit left a lot to be desired. Above it, his bedroom was just that. A bed in a room; although, there was also a clothes rack, which doubled as a curtain and rolled back to display a stunning view over the countryside beyond. So, never mind. He was getting there, wasn't he? The barn was habitable. Surviving the winter there had proved it.

Feeling quite pleased with himself he decided to take Blackie to the pub. After all he had to have a weekend too, didn't he?

Before entering through the heavy oak doorway, he peered through the window, as far as he was able, and heaved a sigh of relief that there was no sign of Nadine.

Nadine was becoming a nuisance. If he wasn't careful he'd find himself agreeing to take her pampered pooch out, just to get her off his back.

'She was asking after you earlier,' said Saul after watching Blackie slump in his customary corner.

'Who was?'

'Princess Nadine,' he replied with a knowing look. 'Time her old man came home if you ask me.'

'I'll have the steak pie,' said Harry, trying to change the subject. 'If there's still some going . . . And a pint of the usual . . . Do me a favour, if she asks again, tell her I've gone abroad.'

'Tell her yourself,' replied Sam. 'She's just coming in.'

Oh no, Harry thought, turning his reluctant eyes towards the door. What had he done to deserve this?

'Ah, Harry, I was looking for you.'

'Hello Nadine,' answered Harry warily.

★ ★ ★

After greeting Jay effusively and briefly proffering a carefully made-up cheek, which Freya found herself pecking, Mrs Hamilton graciously received her bouquet of flowers whispering that she'd put them with 'the others' and deal with them later. Freya immediately felt she should have brought a more inspired gift — but what could you give a woman who had everything?

Jay's mother had cooked a beautiful dinner and was now presiding over the table looking as unruffled and immaculate as ever. 'I know I shouldn't really be cooking on my birthday,' she said, smiling, 'but I enjoy it, so I decided I would. Of course, there are only eight of us tonight so not too large a number.'

'It's absolutely delicious,' said Freya honestly. 'I'm afraid I'm not much of a cook myself.'

'Just a matter of following a recipe and timing,' said Jay's mum with a shrug. 'I don't understand it when people say they can't cook.'

'Oh, well yes, I can cook. But my cooking's rather, well — basic, a bit hit and miss really.'

'Right,' said Jay's mum as though there was nothing right about it at all. Luckily at that moment her attention was taken by another of her guests so Freya was spared from defending herself or enthusing further over the meal, neither of which she felt like doing.

What she really wanted to do was go home and continue relocating any superfluous clutter in the loft, but Jay was obviously enjoying the attention lavished on him by his mother and various of the family friends. *And why shouldn't he?* Freya reminded herself sternly. His sister Jane was there, too, with William, her fiancé who seemed to be quite friendly. Freya wondered whether he sometimes felt a little left out too, but then remembered that one of the first things Jay's mum had told her was that Jane's fiancé was practically a millionaire already. *Jay's unemployed girlfriend versus Jane's millionaire fiancé*, thought Freya — no contest there then.

Later, much later than Freya would have liked, she wished Jay's mum a happy birthday for a last time and made to leave. She knew that Jay would be staying with his parents for the night. Mrs Hamilton had made it clear that she wanted some quality time with her son. Freya took that to mean, time not to be shared with his girlfriend.

'I'll come round tomorrow,' Jay said. 'So cheer up.'

Freya gave a fleeting smile. It was all very well for him to say 'cheer up'. Jay with the well paid job, with the swanky London flat and the safety net of his parents. What would he know about being saddled with a mortgage you couldn't afford and parents who'd put their furniture into store and let their own house out while they were taking a year's sabbatical in Canada? Not that Freya would have worried them for help anyway; she'd been brought up to be independent.

That was the problem really. Although Freya had lots of friends, she felt it was wrong to just dump herself on them for who knew how long?

And actually, thinking of problems, that wasn't really the only problem. The other big problem was the fact that Jay was now taking it for granted that Freya was going to come to London and somehow she hadn't had the courage to tell him she wasn't.

When he'd first arrived, later than expected on Friday evening, she'd put off telling him because he was tired. Then on Saturday morning she'd thought it really wouldn't be a good idea to tell him before his mother's birthday party. But tomorrow — yes tomorrow — she'd have to tell him.

Wearily Freya drove home and let herself into the house, her house — although with packing boxes out everywhere it didn't look much like hers any longer. But she was doing the sensible thing, wasn't she? Renting the house out on a six month let was better than losing it altogether.

Briefly, she wondered how many other girls in her position would turn down the idea of joining their boyfriend in London, in order to stay in the countryside and continue housing a dog, because she supposed, that was what it boiled down to.

Immediately she opened the door Henri hurled herself at her in welcome. A wide smile lit up Freya's face. 'Hello Henri! Who's a good girl then?' She lost her fingers in the silky hair on Henri's shoulders for a moment, then opened the back door and watched as Henri turned herself round in circles and, barking enthusiastically, raced to the end of the smallish garden and back several times. Still smiling, Freya continued to watch. No matter how good the new home would be, she knew it couldn't be as good or familiar as the home she and Henri had created here.

She knew she'd made the right decision. Now, she'd just have to find something; somewhere small, where the two of them could be together. Everything would fall into place. She was being pro-active, positive. Yes, she'd sort something out. Bound to. So long as it didn't involve her going to London, they'd manage — her and Henri — she was sure of it.

Meanwhile she had to work out how to tell Jay tomorrow that, for once in his life, things weren't going to go his way.

6

Early on Sunday morning, Freya and Jay were facing each other across her small kitchen table.

'It's no good Jay,' Freya said again. 'I really don't want to work in London or live in London.'

'A bit late to tell me,' said Jay in a deceptively even tone. 'You're going to make me look a real prat . . . I had to network like mad to arrange those interviews for you.' He looked away and clicked his tongue. 'Opportunities like those don't grow on trees you know.'

Freya bit her lip. 'I know and I'm sorry. But you fixed it all up before we'd even discussed it properly and anyway, I probably won't get either of them.'

'I can't understand you . . . It's not as though I'm asking you to come to New York or anything — although if I play my cards right that might even be an option for me before too long.'

'What? You didn't tell me!'

'No, well, it didn't seem relevant, besides I knew what your reaction would be.'

'Oh, did you?'

'Yes, I knew it would be negative. You don't like change — do you? You prefer to moulder on in your home town and never venture remotely out of your comfort zone.'

Freya looked at her hands clasped tightly in front of her, knowing suddenly exactly why she wasn't going to London. It wasn't so much the change of location that made her wary, it was her relationship with Jay which sometimes felt so tenuous it could disappear overnight.

He could fly away to New York for three months, six months, a year — who could tell? And then where would she be? She'd be stuck in a life not of her choosing in an alien environment. But how could she voice any of this to Jay? He'd made it very clear his part of the deal was to put her up until she found herself a bed-sit, and assist her in finding a job. That was all; that was it. And it wouldn't be his life that would be in any way disrupted. He'd carry on as normal. See who he liked, when he liked. Fly between airports, always knowing that in London he had Freya, conveniently near to his hub of work, and if he wasn't always around — well, so what? Too bad!

'Look, I don't want to argue with you Freya — that's the last thing I want.' He leaned closer across the table and clasped his own hands round hers. 'I care about you.'

When he looked at her like that it was difficult to think straight. She gave a shuddering sigh.

Jay carried on gazing straight into her eyes. 'At least wait until you hear the result of the interviews before you really decide. You'd fit in so well with the London life if you only gave yourself half a chance — I know you would.'

Freya took a deep breath before answering. 'It's no good Jay — I'm not going to change my mind.'

Her hands were suddenly released. His chair grated on the floor tiles as he pushed it back. 'Okay,' he said in what Freya suspected to be the voice he used for business deals. 'You've found somewhere to live here then, have you?'

'Only the cheap, crummy bed-sit I told you about,' admitted Freya.

Jay's eyes narrowed. 'No you didn't.'

Freya clapped a hand to her head. 'Oh no, of course it wasn't you I was speaking to. It was Harry.'

'And who exactly is Harry?'

'He's a dog walker. I met him when I was walking Henri. He charges around with about four dogs; he wears the most awful old combat shorts in the worst of weather . . . A bit of a character really I suppose.'

Rapidly losing interest, Jay smothered a yawn. 'Oh.'

Suddenly Freya felt defensive. Harry had at least been sympathetic to her circumstances. How dare Jay dismiss him in such a high-handed fashion?

'Actually, as it happens, he's very nice. He also boards a few dogs sometimes, too.'

Jay shrugged.

'He even offered to look after Henri for me — if push came to shove.'

'Did he indeed?' said Jay looking attentive again. 'Well, there you are then, Freya.'

'Well, actually no. I've already told you I'm keeping Henri with me.'

Dragging his fingers through his newly styled hair, Jay gave a gasp of exasperation. 'Freya, don't be so fast to close doors — use your intelligence. You've let your house out, right? At the end of the month you'll be homeless. Henri is the stumbling block, right? Now, whether you go to London, or stay here — you have to live somewhere, agreed? At the moment the only place you've found isn't suitable for Henri and you can't bring her to a flat in London, that's a given. This guy is an option . . . Think about it. Don't worry about the expense — I'll pay. No one says she has to be there for ever, but it's plain common sense to consider it.'

Freya blinked hard. Jay was right. She'd be a fool not to consider it, even if only as a safety net. And as safety nets went, she thought, remembering for a moment the lines in his cheeks when he smiled and the warmth in his eyes — Harry would make a good one.

'Where does this old bloke live? You could at least inspect the premises.'

'I don't know . . . Yes, I do. He lives at Mindhurst, you know, near that nice old pub. I've got his card here somewhere.'

'Well, what are you waiting for? Give him a ring.'

'Maybe I will.'

Jay grinned but it was a grin that brooked no argument. 'No maybes — do it right now.'

'You're so bossy.'

'Someone's got to organise you.'

She found Harry's card in the pocket

of her wax jacket, noting as she did so that it said something about him being a financial analyst. Back in the kitchen she found her mobile and reluctantly punched the numbers into her phone and listened to it ring.

Giving her the thumbs up sign Jay picked up his Sunday paper and disappeared into the sitting room.

Moments later Freya followed to find the only visible parts of him were the soles of his shoes propped on the coffee table and a pair of long legs topped by a newspaper with a supporting hand each side of it.

'He said yes and to come now,' Freya said nervously jangling her car keys because she was having second thoughts about this already.

Jay's head appeared round the edge of the paper. 'Well, I didn't mean right now.'

'Too late, I've already agreed. Don't worry though, you stay here and read the paper.'

Jay swung his legs down to the floor.

'No, I'll come with you.'

'I'm quite capable of going on my own.'

'Of course you are but — I want to come with you. Besides, you might change your mind if I don't.'

He didn't see the face Freya pulled behind his back.

★　★　★

Harry had walked the dogs and bought a Sunday paper on his way back to the barn.

It was cold for early May. Not that May was ever predictable. But today felt so dreary.

Once he'd towelled Blackie dry he lit the wood burner, changed his shorts for a comfortable pair of jeans and prepared to sit down with a steaming hot mug of coffee and read the Sunday supplements.

It wasn't long before Blackie padded in from the kitchen and lay at his feet hogging most of the heat from the stove which was warming up nicely. Harry raised an eyebrow at him and Blackie gazed mournfully back but didn't budge an inch.

Harry sighed. He was too soft, that was his trouble. Too soft with animals and too soft with people. Too soft with Nadine. Why on earth had he agreed to look after Za Za for three days while Nadine visited a health spa? Because, he reminded himself, if I didn't — who would?

'You're not going to like it Blackie. From tomorrow you'll really have something to look miserable about. Za Za's going to drive us both mad with her yapping and I'm going to have to mess about with designer dog food in fancy tins . . . '

Blackie continued to look unimpressed and Harry folded his paper to the business section. About halfway through an interesting column on pension options for the self-employed, he was interrupted by the ring of his mobile. Drat, he was so comfortable he was in two minds whether to answer it. But eventually, because he was hungry and had been vaguely thinking of rummaging around for half a pack of digestive biscuits he'd seen earlier, he lifted himself from his cosy chair.

A short conversation later saw him rushing around like a lunatic, gathering untidy heaps of paper into neat orderly piles on the long shelf that acted as a desk as well as a table and ironing board — not that Harry ever did any ironing — well, hardly ever. He checked the bathroom and sprayed disinfectant in the kitchen sink. He sniffed the air hoping the place didn't smell too much of dog. Then, even though it wasn't Monday, he contemplated sweeping up but decided against it as the floor to the barn was of old oak boards and didn't show the dust much. Luckily, by the time Blackie had spread himself over the only rug, which was indisputably shabby, there wasn't much of it, dusty or otherwise, on display.

He folded the paper up then, on

second thoughts, opened it out again to make the place look more of a home and less of a falling down barn.

The yard! For goodness sake, that was what she was coming to see. Forget about the living quarters, if the yard was in a state she wouldn't even want to stay, let alone be enticed into sharing a cup of coffee and possibly a digestive biscuit — if he could find them.

Fortunately, the yard when he inspected it, was reasonable. It was clean, the metal gates and locks secure. There were six separate kennels, each with their own gates. There the dogs would have plenty of room to move around, concrete floors to wear their claws on and a warm wooden kennel each for sleeping. Harry didn't often board dogs but liked to think that when he did, they had good food and shelter. He couldn't have slept had he thought otherwise.

As he turned to go back inside he heard the sound of a car and the crunch of gravel as it drew to a halt on the other side of the gate to the yard.

It was Freya's Mini, he'd recognise it anywhere. So why then, was a tall, lanky, male model type, languidly unfolding himself from the driving seat and looking around the area as though he owned the place? Then Harry's attention was taken by the wide smile of the girl slamming the passenger side door, and he brightened a couple of notches. Ah, it was smiling girl after all, plus, unfortunately, the boyfriend — what was his name — ah, Jay Hamilton, that was it. A Hollywood sounding name to go with his film star good looks.

'Hi,' said Freya somewhat breathlessly. 'Sorry to disturb your Sunday like this. This is Jay. Jay — this is Harry.'

'Hello Harry.' Jay extended a hand and gave Harry's arm such a strong shake he felt it might come out at the socket. 'Freya mentioned your offer to board Henri for a period while she gets herself sorted out. Sounded like a marvellous idea to me so we've come to have a nose.'

'Fine,' said Harry because he couldn't

very well say that actually the plan was that Freya came unaccompanied and they would have a casual, pleasant chat culminating in a cosy cup of coffee in front of the wood burner. No, that wouldn't do at all. 'Come on in,' he said. 'Both of you.'

It didn't take long to inspect the yard. Freya was very quiet and seemed increasingly subdued as Harry explained the regime of the yard.

'I notice you don't have any other dogs here at the moment?' remarked Jay almost as though it was a catch question.

How very observant of you. Take a gold star Hamilton, thought Harry.

Aloud he said, 'No, this set-up was already here when I bought the barn, but I only use it when friends are in dire straits . . . ' Even to his own ears, this didn't sound like much of a sales pitch. There was a long moment of silence. 'It's rather more personal to have them board with someone the dogs are already familiar with.' Ah, much better, he was beginning to get the hang of this now.

'My friends know I'll look after their animals well,' he added for good measure.

Jay looked perplexed. 'Oh, I thought it was your livelihood — your business,' he added just as though Harry didn't know what livelihood meant.

Harry gave a laugh. 'No, not at all.'

'What line of work are you in then?'

Harry gave another laugh. 'Oh, I do a bit of bean counting.'

Jay's eyes were sceptical. 'Bean counting?' He gave a narrow smile. 'How's that work exactly?'

'Jay,' said Freya, placing a hand gently on his arm. 'This isn't the Spanish Inquisition.'

Jay laughed, showing a lot of gleaming teeth. He draped a careless arm around Freya's shoulders. 'Sorry,' he said immediately. 'Just idle curiosity, that's all. What are you doing with the barn? Oh sorry, here I go again . . . '

'That's alright,' said Harry good naturedly. 'Most people want to know. At the moment I'm living in it — just about, and very slowly renovating. The

99

couple in here before me had big ideas but they came across problems — as you do. Then they found they were starting a family. I was looking for a project — so,' he spread his hands, 'here I am.'

Jay was squinting up at the newly tiled roof. 'Did you do that?'

'Yep, the plan was someone would do it for me, but hey, it's all good experience. Got the tiles from China.'

'Impressive,' said Jay.

'Of course,' said Freya, who hadn't been following the conversation, 'I was thinking that Henri would come here as a last resort. I really want to keep her with me.'

'Well, unless you come to London,' said Jay quickly, 'then a good home would be the only answer.'

Freya turned a look on him that would have made most men blanch. He held up his hand in protest. 'What? Well, I was only saying . . . '

'That won't be happening,' said Freya shortly.

'That's okay,' put in Harry swiftly. 'I made the offer — that's all — and now you know it's how it should be, no obvious fleas or smelly corners, you can rest easy that in case of emergency, I'm here.'

Freya gave a sigh of relief. 'Thank you Harry.'

'Look, now you're here, would you like to come in, have a coffee.' Now why had he said that? He might like the idea of Freya making herself at home in his barn but he was almost certain that too much of Jay's company would irritate the life out of him.

'We wouldn't dream . . . ' began Freya.

'That'd be cool,' said Jay.

Harry didn't let them further than a walk through the kitchen which led to the main area.

'As you can see I'm living very basically,' he threw over his shoulder. 'It ain't much — but it's home.'

Blackie hauled himself onto all fours and ambled over to nose at Freya's hand. Obligingly, she scratched him under his chin. 'Hi Blackie.'

Jay's eyes had immediately been drawn to the row of computers on the side shelf. 'Crikey,' he said. 'What do you do with that lot?'

Harry gave an off-hand shrug. 'That's where the beans are kept . . . Now do you both take milk?'

Thinking more than ever that this was a mistake, Harry disappeared into the kitchen and filled the kettle. This Jay character probably only drank coffee made from freshly-ground special beans from an obscure site in the highest altitudes of Columbia. *Tough*, thought Harry as he located the instant coffee jar.

He routed around the cupboard desperately for the half packet of digestives and wondered what on earth he was doing trying to impress Freya with a couple of stale biscuits, when she had this well groomed model standing next to her.

'Sit down, please.' He indicated the sagging sofa which was covered with a couple of very uncool, checked blankets.

'Lovely fire,' said Freya as she sat down. 'I love wood burners — they always look so cosy.'

'Yes, I got that one second hand off a mate of mine. He's gone for a newer model but this one suits me fine. It throws out a massive heat.'

'There are some really stylish enamelled ones on the market now,' said Jay, joining in the conversation.

Harry grinned. 'As you've probably gathered by now, I don't go in too much for stylish.'

'My mother has one,' said Jay.

Not much I can say to that, thought Harry. 'That's the kettle. I'll just see to the coffee,' he said.

There was the sudden sound of a tattoo being beaten on the back door. 'You home Harry?' shouted a voice he would really be quite pleased if he never heard again.

Nadine appeared on the threshold. 'Ah, I see you have company,' she drawled peering through to where Jay and Freya were sitting. 'And wow! Can that be coffee you're making? I'm absolutely parched sweetie; can you spare a cup for little old me?'

'Come in Nadine, why don't you,' said Harry ironically as Nadine pushed past him into the main part of the barn and after brushing off a few dog hairs, sat down rather gingerly in his chair.

'Freya, Jay — this is Nadine, the wife of Nick — a friend of mine,' explained Harry feeling some explanation was necessary.

Jay had half risen to his feet and Freya was staring with undisguised amazement at the vision of loveliness that was Nadine. Reluctantly, Harry had to admit to himself that he didn't know quite how Nadine managed to always look as though she had been freshly plucked from the pages of Vogue, but she did. He'd become used to it and seldom even noticed it now, because he knew that the outside of her covered a mean-spirited soul.

He busied himself in filling the four coffee mugs and arranging biscuits on a saucer. By the time he'd brought the tray in, his three Sunday morning visitors were engaged in a conversation about boats. Since Harry knew that the only way Nadine set eyes on a boat on the waves was through a pair of very expensive binoculars, he didn't attempt to join in the conversation.

Sure enough the talk soon took a different turn and Nadine was explaining how dear Harry had offered to look after Za Za for three days while she indulged herself in her 'one weakness' — the health spa.

Offered? Coerced was more like it, thought Harry indignantly.

'So where is she?' asked Freya.

Nadine turned her head in Freya's direction as though she'd only just noticed her. 'Who?' she asked sweetly.

'Your dog.'

'Oh, she's still in the car.'

'I thought you weren't bringing her till tomorrow?' said Harry.

'Oh, I was passing — it seemed to make sense.'

I bet you were, thought Harry. And I bet you saw Freya's car and thought you'd find out just who was daring to visit me without your permission.

There was no doubt about it, just like the wicked stepmother in Snow White, Nadine had a dark and devious heart.

★ ★ ★

'Well,' said Jay when they got back in the car. 'That was a surprise. I thought you told me he was old.'

'No, if I remember rightly, I told you his shorts were old.'

'Strange sort of bloke, living here on his own; half a dog minding business, and God knows what he's doing on all those computers.'

'I think he's a financial adviser or something, too.'

'Hmm!' said Jay not looking best pleased. 'Goodness knows what sort of advice you'd get from him. He's hardly in the swim of things, is he?'

Freya said nothing, just watched as Jay changed gear a little too early, to her mind.

'What did you think of the glamorous Nadine?' went on Jay. 'Obviously something going on there, wouldn't you say?'

'No I wouldn't,' answered Freya with unnecessary force.

Jay looked across at her with assessing eyes. 'Okay, no need to jump down my throat,' he said.

Freya turned away wondering just why she should suddenly feel so very annoyed with him.

7

Freya sighed. She had only ten days left before her tenants were due to move into her house and still she had no real plan. She was letting the house with basic furniture, and had put her bed, her favourite chair and various packing cases in store.

For the past week she'd been sleeping on the settee and surviving with the bare minimum of possessions. The house didn't feel like hers any longer and by this time she was quite anxious to leave.

Jay was in New York for a fortnight, but that was okay. In fact it was almost a relief.

This morning she'd had confirmation that the job with the financial company was hers if she wanted it. Well, that was easy — she didn't want it, but a part of her realised that she should leave it as an option for the moment. Answering or not answering emails and phone messages from Jay was much easier when there was a time difference, so he didn't need to know about the offer just yet.

After their return from inspecting Harry's kennel arrangements, Jay had insisted on looking at the bed-sit Freya was considering.

The bed-sit was vacant but the landlady, who lived on the premises, was not at home, so they had to make do with pressing their noses against the small window.

'Freya, you can't,' said Jay in horrified tones. 'It's the pits — there's no room to swing a cat. I can't believe you're even contemplating it.'

'Well, I know it's small — but it's quite clean and because it's on the ground floor I thought that in time, she might let me keep Henri here too.'

'This is ridiculous Freya! If you really won't come to London, let me give you some money so you can at least get somewhere decent.'

Freya's expression turned stony.

'Alright then. Let me loan you some money? Please! You can't live here.'

'Jay, it's only because you've been brought up in the lap of luxury you're so horrified. And you know I won't borrow money from you, we've discussed it before. It'll be alright. Besides, I haven't finished looking yet. There's still time to find something better.'

Jay hadn't looked convinced and now, two weeks later, Freya was getting a little desperate.

So, what to do?

She knew that in case of all else failing she could crash on Lorna's sofa bed, but that really was a last resort. No, grotty or not, it would have to be the bed-sit.

★ ★ ★

Harry whistled tunelessly to himself as he locked the back door, crossed the yard, opened the back of the jeep and encouraged Blackie to haul himself in.

The leaves on the roadside trees were almost fully open now, and there was only a smattering of blossom left in the hedgerows. The daylight hours were becoming noticeably longer. Sometimes it almost felt hot. Spring, thought Harry, would soon be turning to summer.

It was impossible to feel low for too long then. There were things to be done to the outside as well as the inside of the barn and if Harry didn't have much of a personal life, well, that was just the way of it. He'd concentrate on the long list of jobs to be done and maybe accept a few more social invitations next month.

Meanwhile he had mates at the pub, his dog walking friends and pretty soon he was going to join a gardening club and possibly pick up some advice on how to deal with the land which went with the barn. He had a fancy to grow his own vegetables and keep a few chickens. That would keep him occupied and stop the ever present thoughts of Freya.

He wondered, but not too hopefully, whether maybe he'd bump into smiling girl this morning. He wondered if she were indeed still smiling or whether she didn't have much to smile about these days. Perhaps she had found somewhere for herself and Henri. He hoped she had, but he also hoped it wasn't a somewhere that included the smooth faced, silver-tongued Jay Hamilton.

Maybe she'd gone to London after all and was enjoying a life of meetings, business lunches, and drinks after work, with smart, edgy office types with their networking skills and way of assessing a person at a glance. Would she feel at home in such a world?

He'd tried it and hadn't. For a while he'd gone through the motions and there was no denying that the financial rewards were attractive, but when the crunch had come and the American company he worked for had made him redundant, the relief had been enormous.

He picked up Butch, the delinquent

boxer cross, from his owner, Jackie, and nodded sympathetically as she recounted in detail the story of Butch's latest misdeed.

'He had me over twice last week,' Jackie said fingering a heavily bandaged wrist. 'I can't seem to control him the way you do, Harry. He just doesn't know his own strength. They told me at the obedience classes that some boxers never do quieten down. They're not really a lady's dog.'

'Oh, I wouldn't give up on him yet,' said Harry. 'I'm pretty fond of him and I've seen an improvement in the time I've been taking him out.'

Butch needed no urging to jump into the jeep and landed in his cage with one easy bound. Blackie watched with silent envy then gave a weary sigh and rested his head on his paws.

When they reached the forest car park, Harry's heart soared at the sight of Freya's Mini. Hooray! Now all he had to do was find her, or alternatively let Butch find Henri whom he seemed to have developed a liking for.

It was wet underfoot and Harry was wearing green welly boots, an old rugby shirt and combat shorts. For a small moment he remembered Jay's country ensemble of designer jeans and sweater and the latest tweed hacking jacket. What a plonker! But then it crossed his mind to wonder how his own outfit stacked up. Hmm, he had to admit it must look as though the only outfitters he'd been near in the recent past had been the local farm workers' charity shop.

Oh well, no good worrying about that now.

He let the two dogs off their leads and prepared to cover the tracks he'd last seen Freya walk.

In the end though, they only made it as far as what Harry had come to think of as Blackie's log. The old Labrador gamely lumbered along at Harry's heels but, on reaching the log, sank down to his haunches and fixed Harry with a stare that clearly said — you can go on if you like, I'll wait here.

Harry eyed him for a moment. Poor old boy was getting timeworn; his muzzle was grey and his eyes rheumy. He patted his noble head.

'Good boy. Stay here, we won't be long.'

Blackie's ears twitched, then flattened again and Harry became aware that there was some excited barking going on over to the left. It sounded rather as though Butch had managed to catch a squirrel or a fox, or possibly even a badger.

Full of foreboding Harry followed the sound.

When he reached the clearing he found Butch looking as triumphant as any dog could look whilst being held with his collar in an iron grip by smiling girl who was talking softly to him.

On the other side of the clearing was an anxious looking lady alongside two black poodles who were giving voice with an ear splitting yap.

'Sorry,' said Harry because it seemed

the best thing to say even though there were no obvious signs of bloodshed.

The poodle lady shot the whole group a look of utmost disapproval before ushering the still yapping dogs away.

Harry grinned broadly. 'We mustn't keep meeting like this,' he said.

'Now behave,' said Freya sternly. 'I was talking to your crazy dog — not you,' she went on as Harry opened his mouth to object. 'You know I really thought he'd go for them then. It was lucky I was here.'

'It was only because they were on a lead and yapping at him. He thought it was his birthday.'

'That's no excuse,' said Freya. Then, looking round quickly, added 'Where's Blackie?'

'Refused to come any further. He's very old.'

'Oh. How old exactly?'

'Well, I don't know precisely . . . He's a rescue dog. That's why he's called Blackie — there was another Labrador there they called Goldie — neither of them had a known history. I got Blackie when I first came back from the States and bought the barn. The rescue centre thought they might have to put him down ... A bit smelly, too old, too poorly, not pretty or cuddly enough to attract a new owner. Well, I wanted some company, and besides he had such a dignified look.'

'Yes,' said Freya smiling and straightening up. She was wearing jeans and a grey shirt that, Harry noticed, almost matched her eyes. She released her hold on Butch's collar. 'D'you think he'll be safe off the lead now? He's fine with Henri.'

'Yes, I'd noticed.' Harry watched as the two dogs greeted each other once more. 'Well, how's things?' he continued as they fell into step together. 'Haven't seen you for a while.'

Freya pulled a face.

'Well, not brilliant to tell you the truth. Only ten more days and we're officially homeless, I'm afraid.'

Surely she was joking. Harry looked

at her profile, registered all over again how pretty it was, then noticed the set of her jaw line. No, she definitely wasn't joking.

'What about the bed-sit?'

'Jay didn't like it. Well, actually neither did I, but beggars can't be choosers, right? Anyway, I looked around a bit more because obviously I wanted to keep Henri with me. No joy! So yesterday I phoned to say I'd take the bed-sit and I was going to phone you about Henri. But, guess what? The bed-sit had gone . . . So it's back to square one.' Her voice wobbled just a little bit and she swallowed and looked away.

Now Harry, control yourself. Just because you'd really like to put your arms around her, to give her a bit of comfort, doesn't mean that's the sensible thing to do. She'd probably smack your face or push you away and you'd never see her again. Don't do it.

Just don't do it!

'Have you told Jay?'

Freya tossed off a laugh which didn't

sound very amused. 'Oh yeah!' she said. 'I've told Jay alright.'

'What did he say?'

'Apart from 'I told you so' you mean? He said that now perhaps I'd listen to reason, board Henri with you and go to London as he suggested in the first place.'

Harry said nothing.

'Then, of course, I really lost it. I told him I'd probably lost the bed-sit because of him, but then that was what he wanted all along, wasn't it? For me to board Henri and go to London. And well, perhaps he'd be happy now I was homeless . . . Not very nice was it?'

'What did he say?'

'Told me I was upset, which of course I was, and he'd be in touch later. I didn't tell him I'd got one of the jobs I'd applied for in London.'

'Oh?'

'But I don't want it.'

'Oh?' said Harry again but with relief this time.

They walked on for a bit further;

Butch covering at least twice the distance of Henri but constantly coming back to check on her now.

'D'you mind if we turn back? I don't want to leave Blackie for too long.'

'Of course not.' Never questioning the fact that they were walking together as a couple, Freya turned immediately to keep in step with him.

Blackie appeared to be quite content when they finally returned to the log. After heaving himself onto all fours and pushing his nose into Harry's hand he nodded in Freya's direction and wagged his tail.

'I've got a proposition for you,' said Harry when they were taking a slow meander back towards their cars. 'I don't want you to answer at once; I want you to think about it.

'I'm a freelance number cruncher. I work from home. After the bank in New York got rid of me and a lot of others eighteen months ago, they realised that they still needed an analyst, but they needed someone they could trust and knew their system. In point of fact — they still needed me. The fact that I'm British helped. The time difference is useful. So, after a bit of negotiation, I still number crunch for them. At the end of the working day in New York the figures come hurtling through — I analyse them and send them back again so they have them all ready for the next day. Now, quite often I'm pretty pushed for time and sometimes it's a struggle for me to fit the dog walking in.'

'Harry,' started Freya. But Harry held up his hand.

'Now hear me out. The thing is, the barn, well, you haven't seen all of it but basically it's divided into three. At one end is the kitchen which you've seen and over the top of it a bedroom and a small but functional bathroom. In the middle is the big room with the wood burner and at the other end downstairs there's a boot-room and shower and upstairs are two more undecorated rooms and eventually there'll be another bathroom. The couple, who had the barn before me, always intended to have that end as a holiday let, you see.'

He looked at her nervously. 'The kitchen end is practically self-contained. And now the summer's nearly here, I could easily move into the other end of the house and use the boot-room shower and adjacent outside loo. We'd have to share the kitchen and I'd have to ask you to look after the dogs I board or dog walk, but it's an alternative you might like to consider.'

Freya had stopped walking and her face was a little pink. 'Harry, you're the kindest, sweetest, of people, but I couldn't possibly take you up on it.'

'Don't say no,' said Harry. 'I've been racking my brains as to how I can manage through the summer. That's when I board the most dogs. And when it gets to six of them plus Blackie and Butch, well, they have to be taken out in batches — it's not easy. You're good with dogs, one of the few people I've met who can control more than one. I'd be so relieved — honestly . . . And you'd have a roof over your head and — think of Henri. You'd be together.'

He'd stopped too by this time and was staring at her speechlessly. Her eyes were swimming with tears. 'I don't know,' she said. 'I feel terrible for telling you all this. Awful, just awful. I mean, I hardly know you. I might be a terrible person for all you know. And . . . and here you are, offering to share your home with me.'

'Freya, you're not a terrible person. You're in a spot of bother — that's all — and we're in a position where we could both do with some help. I really thought I'd have to disappoint people this summer and they'd have to use other kennels that are less, well, homely. Please think about it.'

Freya dashed the back of her hand across her eyes.

Oh, well done Harry, now you've made her cry, he thought.

He took a step forward. 'Look, making you cry was the last thing I meant to do,' he said. Then somehow his arms were round her. His head was resting on the top of her spiky hair, which didn't feel spiky at all he realised, just really rather like soft feathers under his chin. She didn't back off either or smack his face, as he'd feared. Instead she gave a snuffle, looked up at him and blinked.

'You're a good friend Harry,' she said. 'The best.'

And, thought Harry, that would have to do. For now, anyway.

8

After racking her brains as to how to tell Jay, Freya eventually sent him an email. *Owing to bed-sit having gone, have taken Harry up on offer of self-contained unit on the end of his barn and job of kennel maid. Two springer spaniels, liver coloured spots — lovely dogs (Harry's walked them for six months) came yesterday to board for two weeks as their owners have gone to Spain. The weather here is gorgeous. Hope you're having a good time in NY. Sorry I was a bit off on the phone, but things seem to have panned out okay for now. Freya.*

She looked at the email for a few moments wondering why she hadn't put 'love Freya'. Then she put two x's on the end to make it seem more friendly.

Well, they'd never talked about love,

had they? Their relationship had never really verged on the 'serious, planning for the future' stage, it had all been very much on a 'let's just see where this takes us' basis. So why then should she feel so guilty, so defensive, about taking Harry up on his offer? And why hadn't she told Jay she'd turned down the London job?

Anyway, no time to think about all that stuff now; time to take the dogs out with Harry.

She pushed her feet into her trainers. The sun was shining in a cobalt blue sky and there was hardly a breeze. Hooray, she wouldn't even need to carry a sweater today.

With Henri prancing at her heels she went out into the yard. Although only having moved in a few days ago, she'd already fallen into a routine. She rose early, made breakfast which she shared with Harry, then they took the dogs out together. Freya managed Butch and Henri; Harry controlled the springers along with Blackie who took no controlling at all.

When they arrived back Freya cleaned the yard while Harry caught up on paper work. At lunch time the computers started up and Harry ate a sandwich as he worked. Freya did the crossword, before taking the springer spaniels out again.

When she returned she took Butch and Henri for their run which consisted of her walking along the country road at the back of the barn while they were let free in the farmer's field which ran alongside it.

Blackie occasionally ambled beside her on these walks, never deigning to join in the gambolling of the younger dogs. At other times, he was content to attend the solemn business of guarding Harry at work in the barn.

A cup of tea was often on offer when Butch was returned to Jackie, an offer which Freya, finding that she really liked Butch's slightly scatty mistress, was only too happy to accept.

'Harry's such a love,' said Jackie the

first time Freya met her. 'He's been made so welcome in this village. Such a generous person — and genuine too. He'll help anyone out, you know . . . I really don't know what I'd have done without him; Butch is so disobedient when he's with me.'

'You're probably not firm enough with him, Jackie. Firmness and consistency are the important things. I'll come out with you for a couple of sessions if you like.'

Jackie looked delighted. 'Would you really? That'd be great! I'm so glad Harry found you.'

Freya smiled. 'So am I,' she agreed, then felt herself flush because it sounded so heartfelt.

'Now if you wouldn't mind just taking Harry this bread pudding. It's his weakness. There's two pieces there so have a piece yourself.'

Yes, Freya had settled in more quickly than she could have imagined. In the evenings, which were much lighter now, she cooked for them both and Harry had a break for three quarters of an hour or so while they ate together. After dinner Harry had to work again and Freya sometimes watched the television before giving the dogs their final short run. She was almost frightened at how rapidly she'd eased herself into such an enjoyable routine.

Of course, she still had her name down with the job agencies but so far nothing had come up. It seemed that seasonal jobs were being snapped up as quickly as they appeared and the banks and insurance companies were more likely to be reducing numbers rather than increasing them. But the mortgage was being covered plus a bit more, so at least she was solvent.

Humming softly, Freya went out into the yard to greet the springers who were barking madly. Harry was already there.

'Hi ya,' he said with a lop-sided grin. 'Thought we'd have to start without you today.'

'Sorry,' said Freya. 'I was just seeing

to some emails.' Somehow she wasn't quite comfortable with mentioning Jay's name and she noticed that Harry was equally reticent on the subject of Freya's boyfriend.

As they both reached to open the gate between the yard and the gravel layby where the cars were parked, their hands brushed against each other. For a moment as her startled eyes met his, she wondered if the gate carried some electrical charge. Quickly she moved her hand away. It was the first time they'd touched since he had offered her the barn as a refuge; the first time they'd touched since he'd put his arms around her in a brotherly fashion and given her a hug of comfort and reassurance. Ever since that hug she'd taken great care to avoid further physical contact with him because the feeling of safety and relief she'd found in his arms had rapidly changed to something more; something she wasn't sure she wanted to put a name to.

So she ignored the tingling sensation

in her arm, let him push the gate open and fasten it after they'd passed through, then smiled at him as he maneuvred the dogs into the back of the jeep.

'You know, that smile of yours is a lethal weapon,' said Harry, his warm eyes observing her. 'You could melt a man's bones with it.'

Freya felt her face flood with colour.

'It was only an observation,' said Harry, laughing. 'You must have been told before.'

'Not really, no.' Freya walked to the Mini and bent her head to settle Henri in. 'You're picking up Butch? Right, I'll see you in a bit then.'

Suddenly glad to be on her own in order to sort out her confused thoughts, she put the car in gear and took off at speed.

*　*　*

She didn't find the return email from Jay until later that evening when she came back from regaling Lorna with an update on her life as a no longer unemployed, semi-homeless person.

Freya, she read. What on earth is going on? How come you won't move in with me, but at the drop of a hat you move in with a complete stranger?? Rather an odd stranger too! And where exactly is this 'self-contained' unit? I have to say it didn't look very 'self-contained' to me! And Freya — I really don't care if the springer spaniels have red, white, and blue spots or what the weather's like. Just tell me what's going on will you? Jay

She read the email twice. Really, what did he expect her to do?

Jay, she wrote. You're in London most of the time — New York now. I'm here and intend to stay here. I just have a temporary change of address — that's all. I make my own decisions and this seems to have been a good one. Please stop questioning my every move. Freya.

This time she didn't put any x's.

★ ★ ★

The next morning Harry woke up feeling extraordinarily happy. It took him a moment to focus on the untreated beam and raw brick wall facing him, then realise why this was so. Freya, of course — Freya, the smiling girl had somehow come into his life and made the world seem a better place.

For a moment he lay there luxuriating in the knowledge.

His first instincts had been right. She was a cracking girl, not only to look at, she was bright, funny, kind, but at the same time wonderful with the dogs. Even Butch became docile and well behaved when she was on the spot. And she was living here — although not in every sense of the word — with him. Harry could hardly believe his luck.

The only shadow on the horizon was of course, the super glamorous boyfriend. But luckily that particular horizon was geographically a long way off — for now anyway. Have a care though, he told himself, she's living here, but it's temporary. He knew he mustn't do anything to upset the fine balance between friendship and attraction which could so easily, in Harry's case at least, tip over into something much more. Keep your distance and don't presume — that would be best.

Take yesterday for example, when entirely by accident, he'd touched her hand. Her grey eyes had flickered towards his and she'd snatched her fingers away as though she'd been stung. Then, feeling that perhaps her reaction was a little obvious she'd smiled at him with that certain smile of hers that just took his breath away.

He shouldn't have said anything about that smile, he knew he shouldn't, but he hadn't been able to help himself and now the poor girl had retired into her shell and was creeping about the place like a mouse, obviously terrified he was going to jump on her at any moment.

But that was yesterday. Today the sky was blue again, he could smell coffee filtering through from the other side of the barn and he knew that when he emerged from the boot-room shower, which was working very nicely thank you, he'd be able to smell bacon frying too. You're a lucky man Harry, he told himself as he swung his legs from his temporary, fold-up bed.

At breakfast time, although the camaraderie wasn't quite as easy as it had been, the atmosphere was still quite relaxed. After their morning walk, Freya planned to get some food shopping and cook a decent roast dinner for them both.

'You're spoiling me,' said Harry. 'You mustn't think you've got to keep running round after me all the time.'

'I don't,' said Freya. 'I just fancy cooking a roast and it's not worth doing it for one.'

They took all the dogs out as usual, and Harry kept the two springers on their leashes for part of their walk, also as usual.

'They are truly beautiful dogs,' said Freya. 'Just look at them. They're healthy and alert. They're going to win a few prizes for their owners.'

'Yes, I think you're right. They're both eager to please and intelligent and their strength is building all the time.'

The two of them walked along together in a comfortable silence. The other dogs were off their leads but within calling distance, and there was only one other walker in sight at the top of the ridge.

'Pretty perfect morning, isn't it?' said Freya.

Feeling more relaxed and carefree than he had for ages, Harry opened his mouth to agree when one of the springers suddenly saw a flash of rabbit just beyond Freya. The next moment the spaniel had pulled across them both, then kangarooed behind them.

The sudden jerk of the leash bound Harry and Freya in an unexpected embrace. The other springer decided to go in the opposite direction. Freya was pulled even closer to him and for a moment they teetered together in some sort of passionate, completely unrehearsed, tango.

In spite of the frenzied barking, the tangling of legs, and the falling over, this was really rather an enjoyable surprise, thought Harry. Somehow he'd managed to keep a hold on the leashes with his right hand but his arm was bound to his side and in one way or another he'd landed on top of Freya.

A not unpleasant experience as he was fast to appreciate.

He could feel her shaking beneath him. 'Oh God! I'm sorry, are you alright?' he said into her hair which smelled sweetly of apples. 'I can't move for a moment I'm afraid . . . Hang on, I'll try and slip their leads.'

Freya twisted her face so that he could look into her eyes and he realised that the shaking of her body was caused by laughter.

'I can reach them I think.' Giggling uncontrollably she fumbled about with her free hand and managed to release Harry's wrist from the loop of the leashes. 'Now stay!' she commanded the two dogs even though she was still on her back. The two springers, well trained as they were, sat down a couple of yards away and contemplated the pair on the ground with an air of puzzled bemusement.

Somewhat reluctantly Harry rolled away — but not too far. 'Well, that was fun,' he said slightly unsure as to how to handle the situation. Freya turned to face him and burst out laughing all over again.

Delightedly, Harry watched her.

Just how he refrained from leaning over and kissing her senseless was something he never understood.

* * *

Later that morning Freya was singing softly to herself as she unpacked the bags she'd collected from the supermarket. Outside, the dogs started barking and a sudden shadow broke the sunlight that was filtering through the open back door.

'Well, hello,' drawled Nadine. 'What are you doing here?'

Freya looked up, observed Nadine's cat-like expression and wondered briefly what she had to look so narked about on such a lovely day.

'I live here,' she explained briefly to the unexpected visitor. 'Well, rather I lodge here,' she corrected herself, noting the sudden hostility in Nadine's eyes. 'And I work here,' she added for good measure. 'I take the dogs out for Harry and I clean up the yard and feed them — that kind of thing.'

Nadine spent a long moment in looking her up and down before answering. 'Oh, that kind of thing. Cleaning up pooh — how lovely.'

'Suits me,' said Freya serenely. She opened up a cupboard door and put away some tins of baked beans.

'And where does your boyfriend fit into all this?'

'Oh, you mean Jay? He's in New York at the moment. Anyway, we don't live together — he lives in London.'

'Ah ha,' said Nadine. 'So, he doesn't mind?'

'Mind? Why should he mind?' *And, more to the point, what's it got to do with you?* Freya thought to herself, beginning to feel annoyed. 'I think you'll find Harry's busy, but he's through there.' She nodded towards the door between the kitchen and the main part of the barn.

'I was hoping to tempt him out for a pint and lunch,' said Nadine. 'I've been known to tempt him before,' she added with her hand on the latch. 'He's susceptible to a little temptation from me, is Harry.'

Is he indeed? thought Freya at the same time as giving a light laugh which was meant to indicate that she considered Harry's temptations to be his own affair.

'Oh, hello Nadine,' Freya heard Harry say as Nadine pushed her way through the doorway. 'Can't stop at the moment I'm afraid. Right in the throes of serious work. You know me — work, work, work . . . Freya,' he called, 'Are you still in the kitchen?'

Freya grinned. It was such an obvious cry for help.

'Can't leave the computer at the moment,' said Harry appearing in the doorway and perhaps a little too obviously, ushering Nadine before him. 'Perhaps you two would like a coffee or to go for a drink or something?' His voice tailed off to nothing. Freya wondered if he'd seen the horror in Nadine's eyes at the thought of the two of them sharing a drink; then wondered if her own eyes echoed that sentiment quite as obviously.

'Goodness me, no, I wouldn't dream of keeping your new kennel maid from her chores,' said Nadine with a wide smile that was probably meant to take the sting out of her words.

'Actually I was just going to start on the kitchen floor,' said Freya lightly. 'I quite enjoy cleaning floors.'

'Do you really?' answered Nadine in

a tone that said she wasn't in the least surprised.

'Freya, you don't have to do that. You work hard enough already.'

Freya felt Harry's eyes on her, and saw Nadine's lips narrow and her expression grow even more unfriendly. 'Okay,' said Nadine. 'Well, I'll leave you two to argue over that one — count me out. See you soon Harry. Don't work too hard.'

9

Saturday lunchtime at The Speckled Hen was always busy and Freya thought she'd have to wait for some time at the bar before Saul noticed her. However, as soon as he recognised her he came across and took her order for a dry white wine.

'Harry joining you?' he asked, as he placed her drink on the bar.

'No,' said Freya. 'I'm meeting some-one — unfortunately.'

And that was the worst of it, she thought to herself — she was finding it 'unfortunate' that she was meeting Jay. And why had she referred to Jay as 'someone' and not her boyfriend?

A table for two had just become vacant. Swiftly she found her way over to it and sat down, wishing with all her being that this meeting was over.

The last few days had been almost hot and her face and arms had picked up a light tan. Today she'd deliberately taken care with her clothes and make-up, hoping the short skirted denim dress and the unaccustomed brighter lipstick would give her a confidence she was far from feeling.

She was seated facing the door, so when Jay entered with his customary easy self-assurance she was able to watch his eyes search amongst the tables until her found her. She stood up, waved, and indicated that she already had a drink.

He really was impossibly good look-ing, she realised, as he gave a cheery grin in her direction before joining the throng at the bar.

At half a head taller than most others in the pub it wasn't long before he had attracted the attention of the pretty young barmaid who helped out at weekends. Freya saw him mouth his order for a beer and, unable to resist it, go on to indulge in some light-hearted flirting with her. Then, still grinning, he came over to join Freya.

At risk of spilling his beer he leaned

forward and kissed her cheek.

'I'm bushed,' he said as he sat down. 'Flew home Thursday — got to go back Monday. The pressure's killing me.'

Freya smiled. 'Rubbish. You're thriving on it. You look alright to me.'

Jay took a swig of beer and gave an appreciative smack of the lips. 'That went down well! Yeah, you're probably right, I am enjoying it. If it wasn't for missing the beer — and you of course,' he added with just the right amount of charm, 'my life would be perfect.' He glanced at her appraisingly. 'You look well.'

'I feel well — outdoor life must suit me.'

'Think you've lost a bit of weight too — noticed it when you stood up.'

Freya shrugged. 'Probably . . . It's all the walking I expect.'

'Well, we'd better order; I'm starving.' He studied the menu. 'I'll have the bangers and mash. No, I won't, I'll make it the steak and ale pie. What are you having?'

'Caesar salad.'

'Should have known. Don't change much, do you?' He took another mouthful of beer before going back to the bar to order.

'So, how's New York?' asked Freya when, after more banter with the barmaid, Jay arrived back.

'Good . . . Hard work, but I'm enjoying it. How about you, my little farm labourer?' he said, laughing.

'Likewise . . . It's fun . . . I'm happy.'

She felt his eyes evaluating her in more detail. 'Yeah, you look happy. You look — lovely actually.'

'I've picked up a bit of a tan, that's all.'

'So . . . It's no good me asking you if you'll come to London — again?'

Freya sighed. 'Not really Jay. What's it going to take for you to believe me when I say no?'

For a long moment their eyes met. Flushing slightly Freya was the first to look away.

'You don't really want to be with me, do you?' said Jay after a long moment.

'I should have known when you wouldn't come to London in the first place . . . If you'd really cared about me, you would have come.'

Freya's eyes smarted at the unfairness of it. 'No Jay, if you'd cared about me, you wouldn't have asked me to.'

'Oh? And what should I have done? Encouraged you into this situation? A kennel maid? Grow up Freya! This is a step backward on a career path — not forward.' He took another sip of his beer then looked her straight in the eyes. 'You're attracted to this character Harry — aren't you?'

'No! Of course I'm not . . . For goodness sake, I hardly know him . . . But I have to say, he's very nice, very kind . . . '

'He's very nice, very kind,' mimicked Jay. 'Can't you see — he's a loser!'

'How's that?' Freya's voice was dangerously quiet.

'Steak pie?' The pretty waitress gave Jay a flutter of eyelashes as she leaned over the table.

'That's me — yes.'

Freya's salad was placed before her. 'Enjoy your meals.'

'Thanks,' said Freya in reply, thinking that the likelihood was remote.

'You were saying . . . ' she prompted, after Jay had sprinkled a liberal helping of pepper on his broccoli. 'About Harry?'

'Dog walking?' Jay's voice was scornful. 'Bean counting? Living in an old, half-converted barn? Need I go on?'

'I don't think you need to — no.'

Jay directed her, a long, level look. 'I knew he had the hots for you the first time I saw him.'

'That would be the only time you saw him, right? A little early to have made a judgement on him being 'loser material' I would say. As it happens he works from home — for an American bank. Not so very different from what you do, as a matter of fact, only he's into analysis rather than sales.'

Jay's eyes narrowed a little and he paused with a forkful of food halfway to his mouth.

'Has he made a move on you?'

Freya looked at her plate, shifted in her seat and picked up her napkin. 'Of course he hasn't . . . He wouldn't take advantage of the situation.'

Jay gave a snort. 'More fool him: I would. Girl like you — well out of his league . . . Don't suppose he gets too many chances.'

He finished his mouthful and put down his fork. 'Look Freya, try and understand. You're my girlfriend — meant to be.'

'Yes,' said Freya suddenly voicing thoughts she didn't know she entertained. 'And it's all very convenient, isn't it? Me down here, you elsewhere most of the time. In the ten months we've been together, how often have we actually been together? Just you and me talking for instance? Like now? Not often. Not often enough . . . Sometimes I feel as though we're complete strangers.'

In the long moment that followed, Freya was suddenly aware of the background noise of pub laughter and the clinking of cutlery. It was a happy noise with the odd laugh breaking through it. She didn't feel much like laughing herself.

'For all I know,' she went on determinedly, 'you could have a whole string of girlfriends in London.'

Jay rolled his eyes at the ceiling beam above his head. 'Don't be stupid! If that was the case I'd hardly have begged you to join me there.'

Freya looked away. 'That's debateable. You might have decided you'd like your occasional snack of a country girl a little more conveniently placed, like two stops on the underground away. The arrangement was only to be near, but not too near I notice. There was never any talk of my moving in permanently. Perhaps you were afraid I'd cramp your style?'

Jay wiped his mouth with his paper napkin. 'I've never pretended I'm anywhere near settling down — but how could I tell — with you down here when I'm in London?'

'Or New York? Or anywhere else? Well, the truth is Jay, I'm sorry but I no longer miss you when you're away . . . I have a life and I'm happy.' Even as she said the words, she recognised the truth of them.

The rest of the pub was still humming with voices. She glanced round thinking that after only a few days of frequenting this place she felt more at home than she'd ever felt in Jay's stylish flat or any of the designer bars they'd visited.

Half of her was appalled at what she'd just said, the other half recognised that she should have said it long ago. Reluctantly she looked back in his direction. His eyes were on her, their expression unreadable. Suddenly he reached across the table and covered her hand with his.

'You know what Freya? I really believe you are.'

★   ★   ★

Nadine was in Harry's arms and Harry was patting her awkwardly on her back.

Glumly, he stared at Blackie — in his usual position of repose on the rug, as if by contemplating Blackie's honourable countenance he could somehow remove himself from this most embarrassing scene.

Unmoved, Blackie stared back.

No help there then. He switched his eyes to the shivering muddy bundle of blood bespattered fur that was Za Za.

'Oh Harry,' whispered Nadine gazing up at him. 'I'm so glad you were in. I just needed someone strong to turn to.'

Harry cleared his throat and tried to move away. Nadine held onto his shirt with a grip like a vice. 'You should attend to Za Za,' said Harry, inspiration striking rather late in the day.

She gave a pathetic sniff but her grip slackened.

'Sit down.' He cautiously eased himself away. 'Naturally you're upset. I'll make you a cup of tea.'

Making sure to hold her away from her pale designer T-shirt, Nadine reluctantly picked up her little dog, then sat down cradling her, rather distantly, on her knees.

Trying to ignore Henri's whimpering coming from the boot-room, Harry headed for the kitchen and plugged in the kettle.

Just how had he got himself into this position? Just when and why had Nadine set her sights so determinedly on him?

He was well aware that whilst being presentable, he was not track-stoppingly attractive and his personality was well, just ordinary really. He was certainly not made of the material that anyone, setting their eyes on Nadine, would consider as being up to her exacting requirements as a prospective lover.

So why couldn't she just leave him alone?

Was it just that he lived conveniently near? Surely it couldn't be because he was her absent husband's best friend?

Or was it because Harry, unlike every other man she met, did not do a double take at her perfection and bow down and worship obviously enough?

And exactly what was this latest act all about?

He peeked round the door and observed Nadine dabbing at her eyes in case she'd inadvertently smudged her mascara during her dramatic scene.

'I don't think Za Za's really hurt,' began Harry as he turned back again in order to pick up the coffee mugs and avoid her anguished expression.

'Of course she's hurt! You weren't there . . . '

Suddenly the door to the yard which — owing to Harry's fear of being alone with Nadine in a confined space, was already ajar — opened wider.

Freya stood framed in the doorway. Her face was flushed, her hair shining in the sun and her arms and legs tanned and beautifully toned. She obviously had absolutely no idea how lovely she looked.

'Have you seen Henri?' she asked breathlessly. 'I thought she'd be in the yard waiting for me.'

At the sound of Freya's voice, Henri

changed her whimper to a frantic barking which could be heard quite clearly
coming from the boot-room. Nadine,
holding Za Za to her heart as though
Freya was on the point of tearing her away,
leapt forward with fury in her eyes.

'Your dog,' she said venomously. 'Your
dog is out of control! She attacked Za
Za with no provocation what so ever.
Just look at poor Za Za! You should
have that animal put down; she's vicious.'

Oh dear! Harry stood with a mug in
each hand looking from Nadine to
Freya and back again, as though at a
tennis match.

'Don't be ridiculous,' said Freya.
'Henri wouldn't hurt a fly. You must
have made a mistake. Anyway, where is
Henri?' She looked uncertainly from
Harry to Nadine.

'In the boot-room.'

'Well, there you are then. How could
she attack Za Za if she's in the
boot-room all this time?'

'What? Are you stupid or something?'
Nadine was practically spitting feathers.

'She's in the boot-room because she attacked Za Za! You don't think I'm going to watch it happen all over again, do you?'

Freya went even pinker. 'I'm sorry,' she said, 'but I don't believe you. I've never known Henri show any aggression in her life; she's got a wonderful temperament. Za Za must have provoked her.'

'Are you calling me a liar? Ask Harry. Go on, ask him!'

Harry put down the coffee. 'Well, I wasn't actually there,' he started.

'No, but you were looking for Henri, weren't you Harry? You knew she'd got out?'

'Well, I thought she might have. But I also thought Freya might have changed her mind and taken her along to the pub. It's a nice day; I thought they might go in the pub garden.'

'No,' said Freya. 'I left her loose in the yard, but I thought she was too big to get out of there.'

'Obviously not,' said Nadine with a

cat-like smirk. 'She must have squeezed through the fence. I was walking up the lane with Za Za, happily minding my own business when your dog hurtled through the hedge, jumped on Za Za and savaged her. Look at her, she's still shaking with shock — aren't you my poor baby?'

White faced now Freya pushed her way past Nadine and opened the door to the boot-room. 'Za Za must have attacked Henri first. There's no way Henri would have done that, it would be completely out of character.'

Harry watched as Henri, obviously full of vim and vigor, bounded towards her mistress in greeting and Freya slid her hands over the squirming furry body she knew so well.

Nadine narrowed her eyes in triumph. 'See, she doesn't have a scratch on her! You should have that animal put down.'

'Hang on Nadine. That's a bit hard,' put in Harry. 'Let me see Za Za properly. Assess the damage.'

Immediately Nadine hugged Za Za closer to her. 'She's way too upset . . . Can't you see her shaking?'

Harry took a quick glance at Za Za who was now absorbed in licking the blood from her paw. Perhaps Nadine was right and the dog's paw had been bitten in the fight. Or perhaps . . .

'You're right, Henri's fine.' Freya turned stricken eyes towards Harry. 'I can't believe it. I just can't!'

'Well you'd better had, Freya,' said Nadine gleefully, 'because I shall take this further.'

'What do you mean?' asked Freya in a shaky voice.

'Let's just all calm down,' said Harry, unable to bear the look of fear on Freya's face. 'First things first . . . I suggest Nadine that you and I take Za Za to the vet, to look at what's happened here.'

'You don't need to take me Harry,' said Nadine with strange reluctance. 'It's good of you but I wouldn't dream of putting you out . . . I'll take her myself when I get home and I'll let you know the outcome later.'

Harry looked at her through narrowed eyes. Nadine didn't want to put him out? That had to be a first!

'No, it's the least I can do,' he insisted. 'I'm partly to blame anyway if my yard's not secure. The chances are it's only a tiny nick. It looks like a lot of blood, but when it's on an ear or something it always looks worse than it is.'

'You believe her then,' said Freya flatly.

'Of course he believes me — it's obvious isn't it?' spat Nadine. 'No, really Harry! I've told you — I appreciate your concern — it's nice to know someone cares,' she cast a withering look in Freya's direction, 'but I can sort this out now I'm feeling calmer. Thank you Harry for your moral support.'

Harry put an arm round Nadine's shoulders at the same time as glancing quickly in Freya's direction. 'You've had a nasty shock Nadine,' he said. 'I really do insist!'

Trying not to register the reproach in Freya's eyes, he picked up the keys to his jeep and ushered Nadine out of the door.

10

After Harry and Nadine had left, Freya stared at the door for something approaching a full minute.

What on earth had gone wrong with today?

First she'd broken up with Jay which should surely be the worst thing that could have happened and yet had left her feeling sad but slightly relieved; and now she'd discovered that the best canine friend a girl could have was being branded a dangerous animal, accused of viciously attacking another small dog.

And worst of all, Harry believed it! How could he?

Freya bent her head and kissed Henri on the nose. How could he believe that Henri was a killer? Well, maybe not a killer, but Nadine had certainly painted a picture of an aggressive animal carrying out a brutal attack for no apparent reason.

'I don't believe it,' said Freya aloud. 'I won't believe it.'

Blackie gave a long sympathetic sigh which was interrupted by the ring of Freya's mobile phone.

'Oh, hello Lorna.'

'Well, you might try and sound a little more enthusiastic,' said Lorna. 'Life as a kennel maid getting you down, is it?'

'No. It seems Henri's been in a fight.'

'Oh, sorry Freya. Poor little thing, I bet it was a bull mastiff — they're vicious creatures.'

'Well, Nadine says Henri was the attacker.'

There was a stunned silence.

'What? That surely can't be right. She's such a sweet little thing.'

Freya nodded miserably. 'I know.'

'And who's Nadine?'

'You don't want to know.'

'Well cheer up. I've got some good news.'

'Right,' said Freya trying to put a

smile in her voice.

'Two girls — pregnant — at the bank!'

'Oh? Anyone I know?' There was silence for a moment before she squealed. 'Lorna! You're not one of them, are you?'

'Come off it! Mike would have a fit. No, but don't you see what this means? They're going to need a fill in for about a year . . . How about that? Naturally I happened to mention casually that you were looking for work . . . The powers that be loved the idea of having you back. Asked me to sound you out! They won't have to train you and it seems you left a good reputation behind you . . . Of course, it won't be for a few months yet . . . Freya! Are you listening to me?'

'Yes,' said Freya. 'Yes, that's great. Wonderful!'

'So, you won't have to go to London.'

'I wasn't going to go to London anyway.'

'Oh, I know, not immediately, but Jay has a way of getting what he wants. He would have worn you down in the end — you know he would. You couldn't be a kennel maid for ever.'

'Well as it happens,' she took a deep breath, 'Jay and I have split.'

'Oh!'

'It wasn't just because of the London thing either. I just don't think we were suited.'

'I'm so sorry Freya.'

'Yeah well . . . '

'You're much too nice for him. I never really felt you and Jay were right for each other.'

'He was really sweet about it actually.'

'You mean you dumped him? That must be a new experience for him.'

'Nobody dumped anyone, we sort of agreed . . . I suppose I've known for a long time really — that it wasn't going to work out . . . Anyway thanks, thanks for putting my name forward. Tell them yes, I'm very interested. Very interested indeed.'

After a little more conversation during which Freya assured her friend she was fine, no, not depressed, had plenty to do and would catch up with her later, she switched off her phone and looked at Henri. Henri looked back and wagged her tail.

'Okay Henri,' said Freya. 'Now we'll go look for just how you managed to get out of the yard and into the lane, not to mention the field.'

A thorough examination of the yard boundaries uncovered no trace of any gaps that Henri could possibly have squeezed through. Puzzled, Freya even tried leaving Henri in the yard, standing in the lane herself, actively encouraging her to find a way out. Apart from causing Henri and every other dog within hearing distance to bark hysterically, the experiment was completely fruitless.

Surely Harry must know that his boundaries were safe? Why had he taken Nadine's side the way he had? Why had he gone off with her with his arm round her shoulders?

Remembering this last fact with a painful clarity, Freya gulped a sudden lump in her throat.

Earlier, still surprised that she wasn't

reeling from the shock of breaking up with Jay, she'd walked back from The Speckled Hen, experiencing a delicious feeling of freedom.

Optimistically she'd looked forward to spending a lazy afternoon with Harry and the dogs. Now, in spite of the prospect of her old job back, even if only on a temporary basis, she was stuck with a new set of anxieties.

After a sigh she resolutely made her way into the barn and discarding the denim dress, changed back into her working shorts and T-shirt. Occupational therapy was something she'd always believed in.

Ten minutes later she was busily engaged in cleaning the yard. Keeping one ear open for the sound of Harry's returning jeep, she sluiced round the drains with disinfectant. As they were taking a long time at the vet's surgery, she hoped the news on Za Za wasn't serious. Surely it couldn't be that bad? Za Za hadn't looked to be in any distress. But then there was the question of all that blood.

For some reason the memory of Harry's arm round Nadine's shoulders kept reappearing in Freya's brain and the more she tried to shut it out the more compulsive it became to re-examine it.

Perhaps Jay had been right and there was something going on between Harry and Nadine.

Trying to convince herself that it was none of her business anyway if Harry was in the throes of a liaison with the toxic Nadine, Freya turned on the yard tap nevertheless enjoying a guilty pleasure in picturing Nadine in its firing line, instead of the already adequately rinsed yard.

★   ★   ★

By the time a grim faced Harry eventually left Nick and Nadine's ultra-stylish cottage it was late afternoon. He hoped that Freya hadn't let the fiasco that Nadine had staged earlier in the day upset her plans unduly. Then he caught himself on the thought. He'd been right earlier when he'd said he hadn't expected Freya to be back so soon from the pub. So just why had she returned so quickly? Harry was pretty sure that if he hadn't seen a girlfriend like Freya for almost three weeks he wouldn't be content with a quick shared lunch at The Speckled Hen. He'd want and expect to see a lot more of her than that!

Perhaps they'd had a row, he surmised, trying not to feel too elated at the thought. But she hadn't looked particularly upset when she'd arrived at the kitchen door, only mildly surprised at not being able to see Henri immediately. So probably, no — not a row.

She'd most likely come home to get ready to go out somewhere special. Some swanky little restaurant, where the cheapest wine was fifty quid a bottle — something like that. And then maybe over their intimate candlelit dinner, Jay would lean over the table, take her hand in his and, with the dexterity of a conjurer, produce a small square box with a sapphire engagement ring nestling within.

Yes, that would just be your luck Harry.

Having actually, and not before time, rid himself of the pestilence that was Nadine, the smiling girl of his dreams would disappear from his life, in a cloud of white tulle, on the male model of the year's arm.

The corner of Harry's mouth twitched. Finally he was confident that he had convinced Nadine to stop pursuing him. Really, she couldn't have played more readily into his hands.

Once they were in the jeep heading towards the veterinary surgery, Nadine had grown strangely silent. Not even glancing in her direction Harry let her stew — saying nothing.

'I'd rather you took me home Harry,' Nadine said eventually.

'I dare say you would,' replied Harry.

'Well, why are we going the wrong way then?'

'Because I'm taking you to have Za Za examined.'

'But I don't want her examined.'

'I know you don't. 'Why not?' is the question that immediately springs to mind,' he added crossly.

'I don't know what you mean.'

Harry pulled into a layby, switched off the engine and turned to face her. 'Okay, Nadine, I'll be blunt! There never was an attack of any kind on Za Za — was there?'

'What do you mean? Of course there was. You don't think I'd make a thing like that up — do you? Besides what about the blood?'

'Ah, the blood . . . I'm willing to bet Nadine that you have a nice piece of bloody, runny meat in your fridge . . . '

Nadine looked sulky. 'You're crazy.'

'I'm not crazy, but I'm seriously beginning to think you are. What happened Nadine? Were you taking one of your frequent walks that just happened to go past my barn? Did you just so happen to glance in and see Henri waiting patiently by the gate? Did it suddenly cross your mind that no one was around and you could easily take Henri, who's a trusting little dog full of natural curiosity, along home with you? Did you then cover Za Za with some steak blood and make up a dramatic tale of a dog fight? That'd be a great way to drive a wedge between Freya and me, wouldn't it?' He looked at her, his eyes blazing.

Nadine stared at him, her eyes like slits. 'You've got some nerve. Why would I want to do that?'

'Oh, come on Nadine, I know your opinion of my intelligence is low, but d'you think I haven't met your kind before? New York is full of them and I'm not interested! If it weren't that you're married to my best mate, we'd have had this conversation long ago. Leave me alone, leave Freya alone and leave her dog alone . . . You'd better watch yourself if you don't want to turn into a bunny boiler. One thing can lead to another . . . '

'I don't know what you're talking about.'

Harry sighed and went to turn on the ignition. 'Okay. If you're really determined to make a fool of yourself we'll go on to the vet's.'

'Wait!'

Harry leaned back again. 'I thought you'd see sense! Now I'm telling you for the last time — back off. I'm not interested in you. Never have been, never will be. I can tolerate you at a distance, as Nick's wife. But that's it! I don't want you knocking on my kitchen door, I don't want you saying any more than good morning to me unless Nick is with you. Do I make myself clear?'

Nadine was staring straight ahead by this time and she gave a barely perceptible nod.

'You won't tell Nick, will you?'

Harry smiled enigmatically. It was always the same with bullies; once challenged they swiftly deflated.

'No,' he said. 'Not unless you make me . . . Now do I have your word?'

There was a low grunt.

'Pardon? I didn't quite catch that,'

said Harry, determined to make her hate him now.

'I said — yes, I understand,' said Nadine in a tight voice.

'Good, I'll drop you off at your place.'

The journey was completed in silence and the last Harry saw of Nadine was her rigid back as, clutching Za Za, who was busily engaged in licking the last of the meaty blood off her paws, she let herself into her house.

★ ★ ★

Just as she was pouring herself an early, but much deserved, glass of wine, Freya heard Harry's jeep draw up on the gravel.

Immediately, with Henri at her heels and Blackie bringing up the rear, she rushed out to greet him. He looked a little stern faced.

'Oh Harry, I'm so glad you're back. What happened? Is Za Za alright? Tell me I won't have to have Henri put down!'

But Harry still wasn't smiling. 'I'm sorry Freya,' he started once he was through the gate. 'I'm so sorry . . . '

Freya burst into tears. 'Oh no, I can't bear it. I just can't bear it. It wasn't her fault. Oh, surely they can't make me have her put down.'

A pair of strong all enveloping arms came tightly around her. 'What's all this? Who said anything about putting Henri down? Of course she won't be put down.'

Freya tilted her head back the better to read his expression. 'She won't? But you said you were sorry?'

'Well yes, but what I meant was I was sorry you had to go through all that rubbish with Nadine earlier.'

'Rubbish? You mean it wasn't true? But — why?'

'It's a long story. A Nadine thing. She watches too many soaps, she's sheer poison, I don't know how Nick can stand her. Anyway I won't bore you with it now.'

Freya carried on staring at him through eyelashes that were still wet with tears.

'So Nadine made it up. It wasn't true? None of it?'

'None of it,' said Harry firmly.

'None of it,' repeated Freya again, smiling through her tears.

His mouth curved into a smile.

'Oh Harry, I could kiss you,' said Freya and she did.

She didn't mean it to happen. Well, not quite like that anyway. It was just the moment; the relief. And then the kiss changed momentum. One moment it was a kiss of joyful relief and the next moment it had intensified into something else entirely. Heat started pulsing through her and when the kiss ended her heart was hammering so hard she found it difficult to breathe.

What ever must he think of her? Freya drew away, flushed and embarrassed. 'I'm sorry, I didn't mean that to happen. It was only meant to be a little kiss — honestly.'

'I didn't either, but I can't honestly say I'm sorry,' said Harry. 'In fact I've been wondering what it would feel like for a long time. But it wasn't fair. I know you have a boyfriend. It won't happen again.'

'Had,' said Freya suddenly desperate for him to understand. 'Had a boyfriend. We've agreed our relationship isn't going anywhere. That's why I came back early from the pub. I was going to tell you . . . We're still good friends of course, but it seems his life is going to be very much in New York, and mine — well, mine's here.'

'So you no longer have a boyfriend?'

Freya looked back at him. Harry, who had good legs, broad shoulders and an amiable disposition; Harry, who shared her love of the countryside, her love of animals and who she felt she'd known all her life; Harry, in his old clothes with his warm hazel eyes and lop-sided grin. He wasn't what you'd call good-looking, but, oh my goodness, when he looked at her like that her knees went weak and everything felt just — so right.

'No,' she said. 'We were on the verge

of breaking up before I even met you, and well anyway ... At the risk of sounding fickle, I would actually like very much if it did happen again.'

Harry grinned. 'What, the Nadine thing?'

'No Harry, not the Nadine thing. The kiss — stupid.'

'Oh, the kiss. Oh well, smiling girl, I can manage that alright,' said Harry bending his head over hers.

Henri looked at Blackie enquiringly. Blackie closed one eye in a long wink, then went back to the serious business of resting.

THE END

We do hope that you have enjoyed reading this large print book.

Did you know that all of our titles are available for purchase?

We publish a wide range of high quality large print books including:
Romances, Mysteries, Classics
General Fiction
Non Fiction and Westerns

Special interest titles available in large print are:
The Little Oxford Dictionary
Music Book, Song Book
Hymn Book, Service Book

Also available from us courtesy of Oxford University Press:
Young Readers' Dictionary
(large print edition)
Young Readers' Thesaurus
(large print edition)

For further information or a free brochure, please contact us at:
Ulverscroft Large Print Books Ltd.,
The Green, Bradgate Road, Anstey,
Leicester, LE7 7FU, England.
Tel: (00 44) **0116 236 4325**
Fax: (00 44) **0116 234 0205**